O MADCAP DUCHESS

O MADCAP DUCHESS

Pamela Hill

This Large Print book is published by BBC Audiobooks Ltd, Bath, England and by Thorndike Press®, Waterville, Maine, USA.

Published in 2005 in the U.K. by arrangement with Robert Hale Ltd.

Published in 2005 in the U.S. by arrangement with Robert Hale Ltd.

U.K. Hardcover ISBN 1–4056–3270–4 (Chivers Large Print)
U.K. Softcover ISBN 1–4056–3271–2 (Camden Large Print)
U.S. Softcover ISBN 0–7862–7438–7 (Nightingale)

The text of this Large Print edition is unabridged.
Other aspects of the book may vary from the original edition.

Set in 16 pt. New Times Roman.

Printed in Great Britain on acid-free paper.

British Library Cataloguing in Publication Data available

Library of Congress Cataloging-in-Publication Data

Hill, Pamela.
O madcap duchess / by Pamela Hill.
p. cm.
ISBN 0–7862–7438–7 (lg. print : sc : alk. paper)
1. Suffolk, Katharine Willoughby Brandon, duchess of, 1519–1580—Fiction. 2. Suffolk, Charles Brandon, Duke of, d. 1545—Fiction. 3. Great Britain—History—Tudors, 1485–1603—Fiction. 4. Nobility—Fiction. 5. Large type books. I. Title.
PR6058.I446O16 2005
823'.914—dc22 2004029223

. . . and now when the musicians come, they are told it is no more a time to dance.

Calendar of State Papers, Henry VIII, 1542.

AUTHOR'S NOTE

The phrase Madcap Duchess is taken from a play by Thomas Drew, written after Catharine of Suffolk's death in 1580 and performed much later in London in the reign of James I. It is possible that the Earl of Arundel, who is made to say it on stage, did so in her lifetime.

P.H.

1

There were seven of us walking that day in the garden. Five were children of my father by two wives as well as by my mother, who had thought she was a wife when she was none, remaining only Sir John Mortymer's widow. The Pope had since made this fully clear in a bull demanded by the Queen-Duchess for the sake of her own children: therefore, I walked last in the procession.

It was a hot afternoon in late June of 1533, and we were progressing, in our summer coifs and gowns, up and down the paths of the knot-garden at Westhorpe, which my royal latest stepmother had been used to tend with her own hands till she took ill. By now, the precise patterns of the little plants already straggled, none of the gardeners having Mary Tudor's skill.

Frances, the prompt fruit of that royal marriage of my father's which might have cost him his head had the King not loved him so well, was not here today. She was in London as a bride, and I wished her nasty little groom joy of her; she was a big hard creature and not missed by anyone. The marriage had been celebrated with pomp, as if to prove to the world that Frances was after all legitimate despite the scandal at the time. The late ceremonies had however exhausted the Queen-Duchess, who was already ill; and also perhaps she wanted to be excused from attending, as the King's sister, the expected coronation of Mistress Boleyn in September. To avoid offence the Duke my father remained meantime, heavy with office, about the King.

The rest of us, except for little Lincoln who walked as usual with Kate, were all young women, two married and the rest still maids. The King's Scots niece Lady Madge Douglas, who had suggested that we all recite the rosary today for her aunt's recovery, walked in front, by reason of her senior royal blood, with young Eleanor, calling out the mysteries. Madge's mother, the Queen of Scots, would by no means be at the coronation; she was occupied with a young third husband in the north. Behind followed my lesser half-sisters Powis and Mounteagle, both safe within the bonds of matrimony although there had been a battle about the first-named marriage, the date of my own conception having come at an inconvenient time. I averted my gaze from the two prosperous backsides and stared ahead at Lady Madge's swinging fair hair beneath her riding-hood—she had ridden over from Beaulieu—and recalled how not many months ago Madge Douglas had been delivered here at Westhorpe, filthy and almost ragged after living with her outlawed father along the

Borders, having been rescued in time from her mother. The Queen-Duchess, who had heard of the girl's plight just before Cardinal Wolsey's disgrace, had sent by way of him for Madge to be brought south and had herself washed the long, dirty and infested hair with birch-bark till it shone clean, and had given Madge rose-water for her skin, which was roughened with the weather although latterly she had been in brief shelter at Berwick, with the castellan. For a time thereafter Madge had stayed with us thankfully and had been content to learn house-lore and the art of herbs, but was soon sent for to be a companion to the young Princess Mary. By now, the former waif was full of her own grandeur, having ridden over from Beaulieu with four servants in the royal livery. I know why I was jealous of Madge then; she was with Lady Salisbury, the Princess's governess, daily, and I now seldom saw that great lady, who had been very good to me.

'The second sorrowful mystery; the scourging,' called Madge piously, and we rattled on. Whatever else had happened to me I had never been scourged: my mother had only demanded that I be kept out of her sight. Now, the Queen-Duchess was kind; but she had little book-learning and took no great heed to her soul, being more greatly concerned with pleasing my father above all things. She pined for his company while he was away and previously he himself had written of this to the King, begging that he might be permitted to stay at home oftener as it was heavy for his wife when he rode off to obey a summons. However the King craved Charles Brandon's company as he always had, even before the marriage, and like most men insisted on having his own way and being who he was, obtained it. He and my father were physically alike in all things, both big men who might have been brothers. They both loved wrestling and all sport, riding at the tilt and making war real or feigned. It did not matter that my father was of the new jumped-up nobility, his forebears having been traders on the east coast; the King was of the new jumped-up royalty, though nobody said so. Lady Salisbury was of the old. My thoughts kept returning to her.

I myself have the blood of the Nevills, from my mother. It has done me little good except that they remember at times to invite me to their weddings and christenings so long as I remain half-seen. My mother was no longer invited, even by that time. She had been married again, this time certainly, to one Master Downes, who soon ran her into debt: and the man who helped her more than anyone else thereafter to recover some of the money due to her was my father. This shows why so many loved him, as in the end did I. Mother meantime had had a baby by the priest, but that daughter married a baronet. She was called, of all names, Anne.

It is time to explain why I was myself not married by then, at twenty-eight.

* * *

I, Margaret Blakeborn, was Margaret Mortymer then for lack of any better name. As I have said a form of marriage had been celebrated between my parents, a forty-year-old widow with a handsome jointure and a nineteen-year-old youth anxious to make his way in the world; his father had been killed at Bosworth in the year of his birth and he had no relatives of any influence. Charles Brandon at nineteen must have been irresistible, as indeed he remained; but why my mother had not taken leisure to find out that he was already married to her niece Anne Browne I do not know. It is possible that she found herself pregnant and took no further time for thought.

That being as it may, before I came to be born Charles Brandon had been dragged by Anne's kin to Stepney church and forced to renew his marriage vows with her publicly; she had suffered a miscarriage on hearing of his affair with her aunt, and was already with child by him again, his prowess in such matters being unabated. This explains the nearness in age between myself and my eldest half-sister

Anne Powis, as distinct from Anne the priest's daughter by my mother.

Poor mother, groaning in childbirth with me at last after all of the above, had small consolation, at her late age even then, when I came to be born. Not only was I a girl, but I would be hard to marry, as was seen when my eyes opened, one being blue and the other brown. Worse, I had one hand with three fingers and no thumb, a Nevill trait through the generations; they could not blame the Brandons for that. One way and another it was decided that I was accursed like a child of incest, commonly said to be an ape. As I have already said, my mother instructed the servants to keep me out of her sight. It could not altogether be done, and I recall the sight of her, blowsy and already pregnant by the priest, telling me to keep my deformed hand always in my sleeve and to look at the ground, as folk were disconcerted by my odd stare. 'You had best be a nun,' I remember her saying, but I knew even by then that I had no vocation. The priest's daughter Anne proved to have ten fingers. I remember very little else about her, as mercifully, having heard the whole tale, my kinswoman Lady Salisbury, whose own mother had been a Nevill, came herself in her litter and took me away.

I can still remember the sudden great surge of loving-kindness, the first I had ever known, that enclosed me even in the litter as we rode.

The Countess seemed to me like a good fairy, although she was not beautiful except for the twin jewels of eyes in her long Plantagenet face. She wore, as by custom, a stately full hood fashioned of ermine, with sleeves of the same; it was winter, and the litter itself had a lighted brazier in it to keep us warm, and cushions covered in embroidery. I was to find later that this last employment was my lady's great pleasure, but it was one thing in which she failed to instruct me adequately because of my hand. Instead, I was encouraged to read aloud to her while she sewed in her solar; I can remember the incredibly long white fingers threading the coloured silks in and out to embellish a surcoat or a hood for her only daughter Ursula, who was married by then; or else it might be a vernacle, the copy of the Sacred Face as it had been left with St Veronica, for one of the chapels. The long-featured face—my lady's father had been royal Clarence, drowned long before in the Tower—would raise itself briefly to gaze out, as the Countess's ancestor Edward III must have done, towards the Channel beyond which lay France: and would speak to me about what I had been reading, or else comfort me about what my lady knew troubled me still. Her advice was the exact opposite to my mother's. 'Never be ashamed to look any man or woman in the face, Mag; some after all have no sight with which to do so.' I have remembered that saying all my life, and have long ceased to flinch when anyone appears to be taken aback by my unequal stare.

At times I was permitted to play in the two green enclosed places at Warblington which the Countess tended with her own hands, or else to help her do it with my own; this I could contrive well enough, my three fingers having grown strong and thicker on that hand than on the other. When so occupied, Lady Salisbury would cover her grey hair not with the ermine hood, but with a kerchief like any peasant, and encase her long white hands in old kidskin gloves. Sometimes then, or else straight into the solar, her youngest son Reginald would stride in from Baliol, having ridden down; handsome, slim, erect and magnificent, like the old kings he was said to resemble so greatly. I doubt if Reginald Pole ever took heed of me; I used to vanish to my books and leave the mother and son together.

At other times my lady would take me with her on progress. Her estates at that time were situated all over England: Westhorpe was one. She continued my education in all such ways, showing me how land was administered and made to pay, how to keep accounts and run a household, how to make medicaments from herbs as was then done in the monasteries; how to learn Latin, and how to pray. My mother had never taught me this last, despite the priest. When I saw how deeply Lady

Salisbury loved God and had overcome her afflictions thereby, leaving herself with a calm soul, I copied her; and soon God came to me. I helped the Countess also with her charities, her poor folk and her tenants. Later I was to help the Queen-Duchess likewise in this way, though the latter was short of money and at that earlier time of which I speak, Lady Salisbury was rich. She had even supported my father, who had no claim on her, with a pension because Richard III, the Countess's uncle, had killed his father Richard Brandon in person at Bosworth, before Henry Tudor in turn killed the King in the only battle the usurper ever fought.

During that ensuing reign of Henry VII Margaret Plantagenet, as she was then—her father had been Clarence, as I say, murdered in the Tower—was caused, like all of her remaining royal kin, to marry beneath her. The husband chosen for her, Richard de la Pole—he had some descent from Edward III—was kind, they were happy and had children, sons and the daughter. Otherwise, there was tragedy enough, even then. My lady had only one brother, the young Earl of Warwick, who after the death of King Richard should have been heir to the throne. Warwick was for this reason kept in close confinement all his life and stated to be lacking in his wits; but he was never given any education to sharpen them. The Tudor King, pursuing his cautious policy and having spilled his consumptive seed into Elizabeth of York often enough for it to pass to their descendants, waited for an opportunity to despatch Warwick as he had, while abroad, already done to death at least one of the young sons of Edward IV, held in the Tower as they were by King Richard by reason of their bastardy. The younger, Richard of York, was believed by some to have escaped in some fashion, and later a fair-haired man came to Scotland, where the King there aided him and marched south against the Tudor with an army. Perkin Warbeck, as folk called him—he may have been Richard of York indeed or he may not—was eventually taken and imprisoned in the Tower, near young Warwick. It was presently given out that they had conspired together. Warbeck was hanged, as though to prove him of low blood, and my husband's father with him. Young Warwick—he was no more than a youth and had known somewhat less freedom than a bird in a cage—was brought out, without even being told why, and executed instead for the sake of his royal blood; the crowds had never seen him before and moaned in pity, perhaps remembering the old race of kings and suffering already, as they were to suffer still more, from the Tudor's extorted taxes. Warwick being dead, Henry VII stayed to reign, grew rich, then died of his phthisis. His remaining son—the elder, Prince

Arthur, had succumbed to his father's disease—emerged then from the strict seclusion in which he had been kept, began to spend money like water, and married Prince Arthur's widow, a Spanish princess whose father, King Ferdinand of Aragon, had insisted on Warwick's execution before the Infanta Catalina could be sent to England as a Tudor bride. I had all this from my lady.

At first, young King Henry VIII, who had been allowed to know nothing of women except for his dead mother and two sisters, loved his wife. Queen Catharine used her influence with him to try, if it were possible, to redeem the murder of Warwick by granting his sister Lady Salisbury, as she now became, the title, lands, and money. The two great ladies, the devout Spaniard and the equally devout royal Englishwoman, were already close friends. The Countess carried the Princess Mary, the only living child of the King and Queen, at last to the font, and later became her governess. About then, I was taken away by my father, by this time Duke of Suffolk, and sent to Flanders.

* * *

I was broken-hearted at having to leave England and my lady; but she said I must obey the Duke, as she herself had always obeyed God, the King, and her husband. I knew she was a person who could not think other than rightly, and so with many tears I left her, and was taken still weeping across seas to a different life; as different as could be, for my father was at that time paying court to none other than Madame Marguerite, Archduchess of Austria, Regent of the Netherlands, and in fact the sister-in-law of Queen Catharine of Aragon herself, though Madame's own young Spanish husband was long dead and she had since married another, who died also, to her great grief. Her Court was worldly, brilliant, and in its way pious also; it was said to resemble the Courts of Love of the mediaeval romances, but Madame was chaste and so, except once about then, was her young nephew, the Emperor Charles V. All that would have been well enough had it not been for my two step-sisters, who were most unkind to me and had been sent by my father to Madame to be brought up, as their mother Anne Browne was by then dead in childbirth. No doubt they thought I was their servant.

* * *

'Cripple. Odd-eyes. Witch, I'll prick your moles if you've got 'em; where's your cat? Fetch that, do this. Her mother's a known whore.' Powis, who was not married then, later became a whore herself, the talk of the Court when she returned to England; she was my own age. Mary, later Mounteagle, laughed, showing her pretty teeth; our father was always fondest of her, for Anne's birth had killed their mother. 'Maybe,' said Mary, 'she's the priest's child and not the Duke's. It happened after, why not before? Get off the chest, you Mag, I want my gown; you can have them iron it. There's dancing tonight, but who'd dance with you? Witches in a coven, maybe.'

I was rescued from all this when Madame began to notice me, seeing for herself perhaps that I always looked miserable. They say she was in love with our father and even dallied at one time with the thought of marrying him, but I remember her always in widow's weeds for her dead husband Philibert of Savoy, with a white pleated barbe under her heart-shaped chin and the Hapsburg lip thrusting out above as if stung by a bee, and her eyes sleepy and laughing. She did, though allow a lock of her beautiful fair hair to stray out from under the widow's coif; that might have been for dalliance, or perhaps vanity. She had agreed at any rate to bring up my two half-sisters, and now myself to wait on them, at the Duke's request, so she must have favoured him a little at the time he and the King were over together at Térouenne making war on the French. There were tales about a ring my father had slipped on Madame's finger, and she laughed and took it off again, or perhaps it was the other way round; but King Henry in his heavy boisterous way made more of a jest than was needful, and Madame, proud of her ancient blood, made it clear to everyone that she had never considered marrying an upstart, and never would. However she began to favour me, not as Charles Brandon's daughter but as someone who, as she soon found, could read Latin with her, as I had done daily with Lady Salisbury; and Madame, among her talents for governance which in the end brought about peace, had time nevertheless to be a scholar. I would stand at her lectern daily, and spent less time with my half-sisters than before; in the end they returned to England to be married there, and I stayed thankfully on. 'God tries us for our own good,' Lady Salisbury had told me, and now perhaps my trials were over. I followed Madame like her shadow or her dog, and learnt much worldly wisdom. Later, when she became ill, I nursed her; she had never in fact fully recovered from the birth of her dead child by the Infante, long ago in Spain.

* * *

We were still walking about the Westhorpe garden that day I remember, and Madge was coming to the end of the sorrowful mysteries. The summer sun grilled down. Mounteagle wore a gown of blue sarcenet and Powis a tawny. Both had their hoods pinned up in the new crosswise fashion of Mistress Boleyn, who had also designed hanging sleeves to disguise her devil's sixth finger. Perhaps a deformed hand did not after all prevent one's advancement. They said the King had been bewitched now seven years, but had bedded the Boleyn at last and she was duly pregnant by him; therefore, there was the coming coronation. Queen Catharine was however still alive.

*   *   *

'How is my Lady Salisbury?' I had said to Madge when she arrived with her four servants. She had told me that good lady was well, and the Princess Mary also. The Princess and Madge were friends, being close of an age. Madge I knew pinned gold saints' images about her bed-curtains at night; she had carried them with her all through the difficult Border times, as though they made her feel secure.

*   *   *

I can remember the pale grave young Emperor, to whom Princess Mary was at one time betrothed. When it was known that he might marry into Portugal instead, they say it was her first sorrow; she sent him an emerald for constancy, to wear and remember her by. She was a child then. Even now she was still kept as a child, told nothing as yet of the King's intent regarding her mother. I saw the Princess more than once, both times playing the lute rapid Spanish-fashion under the trees at Beaulieu. She spoke Spanish from her mother, almost better than her own tongue, and like many Spanish women had a deep harsh voice, but could sing well. Her Latin was better than mine; she was kept hard at it by Queen Catharine, who had in turn been kept hard at it by her own mother Queen Isabella of Castile, the one who made war like a man.

* * *

War with France and England had ended with the King's young sister Mary sacrificed to old Louis XII, but she danced him into his grave in eighty-one days. She had been in love with my father before leaving England, and he was with her in France and they were secretly married almost before the old King was cold. Mary Tudor had been the finest prize in Europe and should have gone to the Emperor thereafter, but wept and clung to my father although they say the new King of France had tried meantime to ravish her. The returning pair were pelted with stones by the angry folk of Calais, who by no means approved a marriage for love if it deprived them of privileges. Nor, on the face of it, did King Henry, though they say he connived at it: but he made my father repay every penny of the French dowry, which kept the pair in debt for life. Frances was born soon, as I have said, and then Eleanor and the two boys. As by that time it had become clear that Queen Catharine would bear the King no more children, the Queen-Duchess—the French queen, as the country folk always called her—petitioned the Pope to ensure that my mother's marriage to my father had never been valid, as mother was inconveniently still alive, with Master Downes. I was in Flanders at the time, and did not greatly heed any of it. It did little good, for null and void my mother's Brandon marriage might be and have always been, but the French queen's elder boy died of the Tudor wasting sickness, and now the Queen-Duchess had it herself.

Madame died also, and after that I came home. It was strange to see the unknown children running about Westhorpe, which I remembered from the days of Lady Salisbury. Now it had been taken from her, with many other things. Mistress Boleyn did not favour those who remained friends of Queen Catharine, and showed it in small needling ways till she could achieve large ones: that time was, however, to be short.

* * *

Lincoln, the remaining Brandon boy, walked now beside Kate Willoughby my father's ward,

Lincoln's own betrothed. I was fond of pretty little Kate's sharp wit; Lincoln adored her. His spindly legs moved now close against her skirts, made of rich silk as Kate was an heiress. My father had been unfortunate with an earlier rich ward, the Lisle girl, who on growing to full age had refused to marry him, to his mortification. That had been before the royal love-match, and the matter was never now spoken of. Lincoln was gazing up at his betrothed, who though not tall was taller than he; he was ten, Kate thirteen. I thought how of all the well-found young creatures who walked before me there were none whose futures were not now assured, most things having been arranged by the Duke; he was grown a prudent man since his marriage and, by now, a wise one. There had as I say been a small difficulty about Powis' legitimacy, as her groom had likewise been my father's ward and his family said young Powis had been hastened into it; but there it was, duly consummated. Young Eleanor was still unprovided for, but it would not be long. A claim to the throne is an asset, and Eleanor had been spoken for in Spain; but matters were uncertain with regard to that country because of Queen Catharine's refusal to be divorced, and my father had exercised his prudence accordingly, saying Eleanor must be married after all in England, when it should befall.

2

Kate Willoughby's mother was a strong-minded Spanish noblewoman named Maria de Saliñas. As a young woman she had come from Castile to replace an earlier attendant of Catharine of Aragon, who was still at that time Princess of Wales, Prince Arthur's widow. They had known one another at the Court of Ferdinand and Isabella in childhood and, then or later, became close friends for life: Catharine could inspire such devotion, as also from my lady. Maria, who was handsome like all the young Spanish women sent to England—old Henry VII had insisted that they be so in order that they might marry early and he himself be free of their charges—Maria found herself a husband soon, a widower of ancient title with great estates in both Norfolk and Suffolk, Lord Willoughby de Eresby. They had two sons who died, and Kate, called for the Queen, who lived.

Her father died early and Maria herself did not marry again. She in any case preferred Catharine's company to all other, and after Henry VIII had married his brother's widow was often about Court. When at home, she pursued a running battle with her brother-in-law about little Kate's inheritance. Being tenacious, in the end she won it; but meantime it was best to put Kate in ward, and my father was chosen, being by then married to the King's younger sister and able to have his less fortunate wardships forgotten. The Queen-Duchess was kind to little Kate, as she was kind to everyone; Kate's ready wit amused her and my father, and the child in any case was a pleasure to watch, graceful and small as a fairy after big-boned Frances, apt of tongue after silent Eleanor, worshipped by Lincoln to whom she was shortly betrothed, as such a marriage would in time be suitable for everyone; at least, so it was thought then. My father the Duke used to watch Kate with delight, jest with her, tease and play with her far more than he did with his other children; she loved him like the father she had hardly known, and diverted the sire of many daughters more than his own ever did: they mostly plagued his good-nature, and he was disappointed also by the death of the elder boy, knowing the younger to be lacking in spirit. Young Lincoln himself could never stay far from Kate, watching her always as if she had been a fairy, with her great dark eyes and shining hair, and he under her spell; then she would tickle him or make him dance, for she was light of heart in those days, or else they would play battledore. Kate always won, as Lincoln had no physical prowess to speak of, to our father's chagrin. Lincoln was not a Brandon but a Tudor, of the delicate breed

Prince Arthur himself had been; apart from the splendid King, who took after his Plantagenet grandfather Edward IV, these young Tudor males were like weak plants, and died early out of the sun. I looked now at the boy's white neck upthrusting like a thin underfed leek between his cap and collar, and prayed that he might have health enough to make Kate happy when he came to be her husband.

'The fourth sorrowful mystery, the Way of the Cross,' called Lady Madge, who would never lose her Scots accent so that the r's rolled always. I tried to think of the prayers, then of the dragging way through the crowds in the narrow Jerusalem streets. None of these, not the scourging, not the Crucifixion itself, was as bad to my mind as the Agony, when Christ knelt alone on a rock waiting for betrayal, and the disciples slept. I did not look down at my maimed hand, managing the beads ably enough as it did most things by now: having the blood of Warwick the Kingmaker in me had brought me my own cross, but there are worse ones. I could after all disguise the hand in Mistress Boleyn's fashionably hanging sleeves; and instead of thinking of the dying Queen-Duchess I thought now instead of that enchantress of a woman, whispered already to be somewhat less in the King's favour than she had been now that he had possessed her body at last. The Boleyn had danced, and had made the King dance also to her piping, alienating him from his wife and daughter, pinning up the long hoods the Queen and Lady Salisbury wore to make a piquant distraction from the swelling on her neck. She had once loved a young man and he had been taken from her; and one day, like us all, she would die in some fashion. The Queen-Duchess would however die first and I firmly made myself think of her; prayers or none, she would not recover. My lady would have told me not to grieve that so good a woman was going to God. Her own brother Warwick was already there in his innocence, and no doubt her husband also; she had daily Masses said for them both.

My mind fixed itself on the remainder of the rosary, and we were at the glorious mysteries before I had a vision again of the little Princess Mary at Beaulieu, reading her Latin daily and playing her lute, with the rapid skilled fingers that had used to delight her royal father. The King never rode to Beaulieu now. What would happen when the Boleyn's child was born?

* * *

When the rosary was finished we broke up into groups. Madge Douglas turned back from Eleanor and came to where I stood alone on the path. Since her own brief stay at Westhorpe she had allowed me to become her friend, Queen of Scots' daughter or not; no doubt the fact that we both had mothers who neglected us, and had made rash later marriages, gave us some matter in common. Misadventure however made Madge herself unduly conscious of her royal origins; she maintained a queenly manner even now. I asked her quietly how matters fared at Beaulieu, and Madge looked grave.

'Nothing is known for certain,' she said. 'My Lady Salisbury bids us pray always that the worst may not happen regarding the King's matter.' Her blue eyes glanced cautiously about to ensure that none overheard; the matter of the divorce was not spoken of by anyone. 'The Princess knows nothing yet; my lady guards her while she can,' Madge added in the tone of a much older woman than one not yet twenty. 'Perhaps the King may remember how greatly he once loved her, and perhaps again love her mother,' she added, but I doubted that; Queen Catharine was the best of women, but had taken too much heed to her soul all her days to care for her body, and the King was after all a man in a witch's thrall. I remembered the pale Emperor, and how his holding prisoner of the Pope alone prevented the divorce of his aunt the Queen from being made fact. Royal divorces were not new; old Louis XII had long ago been permitted to discard his first crippled wife, Jeanne of France, who had resisted as fiercely as the barren and stoutening Queen of England was resisting now. It was perhaps a judgement on Louis that his vaunted second marriage to Anne of Brittany had produced only daughters who could not inherit France, and that he should have been danced at last into the grave by the young third English bride who now lay indoors dying.

'There is someone coming,' said Madge. It was Slyfield, the Queen-Duchess's usher, hurrying out of the new wing with its royal crenellations at the top, moving silently as a good trained servant should, but with his eyes on me; I knew it was urgent. I made some excuse to Madge and went straight to him.

'Mistress Mag . . . my mistress . . . Her Grace . . . it is the end, I think, or near. She would speak with you; pray come.'

* * *

I picked up my skirts and hurried in beside him, through the door and into the further chamber. Before entering I could smell the lavender being burnt in shovels, as had been done since the beginning of the illness. Otherwise the air grew foetid with lung-rot. They had closed the shutters and drawn the bed-curtains as if for a lying-in: yet it was not birth here, but death. The chaplain moved already in the bed's shadows. On the bed itself lay Mary Tudor, Queen Dowager of France, Princess of England and Duchess of Suffolk, second daughter of Elizabeth of York, my father's wife aged thirty-six. Her face was in shadow, but the long throat, transparent now with illness till it seemed blue-white like a hyacinth stalk, showed above the covers. On the wall hung a portrait of the Queen-Duchess as she had been when my father's bride, staring proudly out at beholders while her hand lay in his, his big solid bearded frame contrasting with her own fair delicacy; the great-eyed oval face, the tiny Plantagenet mouth the King had also inherited, the smooth silver-fair hair confined in its round hood. That hair Mary Tudor had got from her mother, who should have reigned as Queen and was in her lifetime much beloved. So had this woman been, whose breaths now came raucously and with difficulty. I knelt down by the bed and kissed the hand with my father's ring on it; the flesh was transparent and the ring hung loose.

'Madam, how do you? What may I do for you? My father will soon ride home.'

I said this to comfort her; he would come as soon as he might, I knew, but it could hardly now be in time. The Queen-Duchess turned her head a little and I could see that they had swathed it in a linen coif against the sweat of long illness. She had once been the most beautiful woman in Europe, enchanting the old King of France in her youth till he danced once too often; now, her face was that of a skull, but the eyes spoke still, regarding me with great kindness. A trace of blood came from the corner of her mouth as she struggled to speak. I took a cloth and wiped it gently away.

'Sweetheart Mag.' Her face smiled a little; I could hear the whisper she still contrived. 'I must ask . . . forgiveness . . .' Her voice broke then and her words puzzled me.

'Forgiveness, madam? You have used me with all kindly love. I came as a stranger, and you made me at home.' I knew she could have resented me, as a further reminder of my father's multitudinous early begettings; but she had not, any more than she had resented Anne Browne's daughters, who used her with as little respect as her own children did, in particular Frances, who herself resented not being the Emperor's daughter and despised her mother's preferred marriage to a commoner, our father. I kissed and fondled Mary Tudor's hand again and held it against my cheek to give it warmth; the dying are cold already, in their hands and their feet. She returned my caress with as much pressure as her strength might still contrive. The muscles of my cheek curved against the thin cold hand as the Queen-Duchess spoke once more.

'For . . . the bull. The Papal bull. I . . . did not ask for it to harm you, and had I known you then . . . might not, and yet, it was for the sake of my children by my lord.' Her voice grew strong suddenly with pride. 'I had to prove myself Charles Brandon's true wife before the world. It was more for this than . . . than that, with the Queen like to bear no more children, mine might . . . one day rule England, but my sister Margaret's girl would come first, yet England . . . hath never had a ruling queen since Maud, and she had to escape in her nightgown.' She fell to laughter, then to coughing, and again I had to stanch the blood. It came more strongly now, and soaked the cover darkly. 'Dear madam, do not trouble any more.' I begged. 'You must rest; soon the Duke will come.' I knew well, unless he was already at the door, that it was too late. I had sent Slyfield at once to order riders in utmost haste to London; even the King must heed this news and part for the time with his preferred good fellow. I spoke then into her ear; they say the hearing goes last, and I spoke clearly. 'No one doubts that you are the Duke's true wife, and that he loves you well,' I said. The chaplain came closer; I knew it was time for Mary Tudor's last confession, after which she must speak with none but God. Yet she talked on, as if leaving this world, with my father still in it, was what she most regretted, uncaring either for herself or her soul.

'Tell my dear lord I love him more than my life. They would have stoned us that time in Calais, but I would do all again. Tell him . . . I love . . .'

The blood gushed up again finally, and the priest motioned me sharply away. I knew that when the Duke came it would be to learn that his royal wife was dead. I went out again into the sunlight Mary Tudor would never again see, and myself gave the news to the rest. There had been no time to send for them.

* * *

After the Queen-Duchess's body was shriven I helped the women make her seemly for her husband's coming. I myself combed out the sweat-darkened hair and sponged it carefully with sweet essences until it had dried out again to its silver-fair sheen. When it flowed over her shoulders and breast like a shining veil I thought of the other dead women who had had such hair. The Plantagenets had from early times been golden; and Elizabeth Woodville, who had beguiled Edward IV into marriage and thus angered my great-uncle Warwick the Kingmaker to betrayal and death at last on the field of Barnet, had herself been known in her time as a silver-fair beauty of great virtue, although like Anne Boleyn's enemies hers said she was a witch. My own Madame, in Flanders, in her youth had had flaxen hair, long and waving, from the old Austrian Hapsburgs her forebears; her father Maximilian had worn it always loose to his shoulders. When Madame lay dead, as the dead are again beautiful for a time, it was possible to see once more not the ageing woman puffy with long ill-health, but the fair-haired princess who had aroused such passion long ago in the Infante Juan that he died of it. Her life's work was done then, and peace made with France. I recalled how she had taught me many things I would never have learned from Lady Salisbury, who kept her soul close; the world's wit, the languages spoken daily about that polyglot Court where the Emperor himself was ruler of Spain and Austria and the Americas and half the world. Spanish, Flemish, German, Italian, even French were spoken there despite the long wars. I learned them all.

Fair hair. I had heard the story of how Madge's mother the Queen of Scots had ridden at fourteen through Edinburgh at her first bridal to James IV, her long hair loose from his saddle-bow; and later, at the English Court, she and Queen Catharine and my Queen-Duchess had all three let down their long rich tresses of silver-gold and reddish gold and had gone thus to the King to beg him to spare the young 'prentices who were being hanged about London, and he granted their request. Mary Tudor looked a little now as she had perhaps done then, her dead face grown smooth though the flesh still clung to the bones. She lay ready for my father in cloth of gold tissue, like a queen; yet she had been queen in fact to none but old Louis XII, and that against her will. After he had died and she was alone in white dule, the new King of France, Francis Foxnose, came into her mourning-chamber and tried to ravish her as I have said, unwilling that such a prize should go to his rival the Emperor and hoping his own wife Claude would die suitably in childbirth. Mary Tudor had resisted him by confessing her love for my father; and Francis then aided the marriage.

It had been happy, despite the dowry repayments insisted on by England's King. I knew that his wife's dying in his absence would cause my father great grief.

*　　*　　*

By the evening, when it was still light, we heard hooves clatter in. My father had arrived in haste, with many horsemen. His great bulk stood within moments in the doorway of the death-chamber, still with his basnet on his head; he swept it off, as did Frances' puny bridegroom Dorset, who had ventured in behind him. Frances herself would no doubt follow at leisure. I watched the Duke stride forward and kneel by his dead wife's bed, trying to take her hands from the crucifix about which they had already stiffened, then kissing them for a long time where they lay placed. I saw the whitening hair above my father's thick neck as he knelt, and felt compassion for him. Despite his grief, his presence filled the room tremendously, like the King's would do. Idly, in the way my thoughts often rove, I recalled how it had always been necessary for my father to permit King Henry to win in tourneys he could have won for himself, lest the royal jealousy be aroused. Caution was necessary with our monarch, even among his closest friends; overnight they could become victims, as Buckingham had done, having been brought up in Henry's own chamber from the time they were boys together. Now Buckingham's head was off his shoulders, the excuse given being that he had raised royal crenellations on his private abode, as we had lately done at Westhorpe. One must keep watch always.

The Duke's grief now was real, with tears coursing down his bearded face. I remembered at one time seeing, without meaning to do so, that scrap of his handwriting in a letter to the King, trying to excuse himself from attendance at some Court function or other which took him away. *It will be hevy for my wife.* My father was a kind-hearted man, for all his steady desire of preferment; unlike the cold-hearted Norfolk, his unfriend, who was equally ambitious but used his own wife abominably. Charles Brandon, Duke of Suffolk, was forty-nine years old, widowed in the prime of his life. It was probable that he would remarry: the thought came to me even so soon.

I knew that I had great affection for my father and would endure this. He had treated my mother ill, but the reason then had no doubt been money; since, he had tried to help both her and myself. I would do as he bade me in all ways. I was, after all, his eldest daughter.

Madge Douglas came in then gravely to view her aunt's laid-out corpse, with the others filing behind her. Kate and little Lincoln came last, he wide-eyed with grief for the loss of his mother, though it had been long expected; but a child is slow to accept change. Lincoln loitered in the shadows beyond the bed, having given way as usual to shyness in his father's presence. Suddenly the latter's great bulk heaved itself to its feet and the Duke, the tears still wet on his face, turned about to where Kate Willoughby stood calm-eyed by herself: she was not one to weep and had seen death before, her father's when she was a small child, and that of two baby brothers previously.

'Little Kate, you are all my solace now.'

The familiar voice came thickly. My father groped for the young creature and took and held her close in his arms against him, much as a child would cradle a doll for comfort. Kate's smooth silky hair spread itself contentedly across his riding-coat. I think I knew already what would happen: and saw young Lincoln, his face grown white as the dead woman's, standing by and staring, his mouth slack as an idiot's with sudden shock. I turned my head and looked at young Eleanor Brandon, whom for the moment nobody much heeded. She, at least, was crying for her mother.

* * *

Frances arrived shortly, too full of her own consequence as chief mourner to pretend a grief she did not feel; she had never shown affection for the Queen-Duchess. At the funeral she rode ahead of everyone on a horse with long black velvet trappings, led by a page in livery: the rest had black cloth only. By then, there had been the lying-in-state in Westhorpe chapel, three weeks long, so that the embalmed corpse had ceased to resemble flesh so much as wax, the tiny mouth grown prim and withdrawn in the smooth dead face. The mourners were all women, as was customary then: the obsequies of Elizabeth of York, the Queen-Duchess's mother, who had died in childbirth thirty years before, were copied to the last detail, proof of the dead woman's own royal blood. Queen Catharine herself, whom Mary Tudor had greatly loved, was not permitted to be present. The former's every movement was watched these days, and her popularity with the common people might have caused rioting had she been seen abroad, for rumours about Mistress Boleyn's pregnancy were by now rife in England and abroad. Lady Willoughby, the Queen's close friend, however came, and rode beside her daughter, their walking escort holding the horses' heads. I myself was seated behind in one of the mourning-coaches. Ahead in the procession I could nevertheless see the hundred poor men carrying their candles, and the long bright blaze of escutcheons hung all the way from the Abbey's great brass main gate to the inner high altar itself. The people lined the roads to bid farewell to the French queen, as she was always known among them. Some were in tears, some merely stared at the show.

The Abbey at St Edmund's Bury was at that time almost a city in itself. Its gates, towers and high walls still stood proudly, as they had done from early times after St. Edmund's murder. Soon they would be thrown down, and even the Queen-Duchess's tomb destroyed, though her body was later reburied by the King's order. Meantime, it lay before the high altar all through the night, with prayers said and sung: and next day we all, Madge Douglas leading us, went up in turn with our offerings, these being layer upon layer of gold cloth; by the end, the corpse was covered. I stared up at the Queen-Duchess's motto *La Volonté de Dieu me Suffit*, and thought how if it had been true she would have been married to the Emperor and not to my father. Then I watched as little Kate Willoughby and her mother returned together down the altar steps, having knelt there with their long trains disposed by their waiting women. It was privately known, even by then, that Kate would be married to my father at the summer's end.

3

After the marriage I obtained my father's permission to return to Beaulieu for a time. There were several reasons, some of which he no doubt guessed at with his accustomed shrewdness. I knew well enough that the consummation of marriages to very young girls took place; Henry VII's scholarly mother Margaret Beaufort had been eleven years old when she bore him. Nevertheless it was not natural to me to think of a child in the bed of a man almost four times her age, and married often before, moreover so recently widowed from a wife he had loved. The haste in consummation sprang I knew from that earlier failure, one of Charles Brandon's few; the fact that, as I have stated, he had once upon a time had the wardship of the young Lisle heiress, and intended marrying her when she should come of age, at which point the heiress herself flatly declined to have him for her husband. This time, with Kate, there was to be no such doubt, although Kate was so fond of the Duke there might still have been none had he waited. I do not doubt however that my father handled her kindly, using the playful teasing way he always had with her, and she seemed happy enough the day after, before I rode off. I loved Kate and I loved my father, and wished them happy, which they doubtless were.

Another reason for my going was the presence of Lady Willoughby. That strong-minded Spaniard, having won the battle over her daughter's inheritance, made ready to see to it that the new Duchess of Suffolk should become mistress in her own houses, of which there were several; the Barbican in town was one, and later on we all went there together often. Nevertheless during the Queen-Duchess's illness I myself had held the reins of the household to a certain extent, and it was clear that Maria Willoughby wanted me out of the way, which was natural enough. She spent more time with her daughter than in former days, for the Queen was no longer at Court, kept separate by now as she was from her friends and her daughter. I learned more of it all when I reached Beaulieu; but before going off said farewell to little Lincoln, who was still dazed by events and never in fact recovered from them. I heard later that from that time he ceased to pay any heed to his lessons, lacking Kate to share them with him; neither the resulting whippings from the tutor nor any other thing would make the boy pay heed to anything; he pined away, having nothing left for which to live. I heard of his death within the year, when Kate was three months pregnant. Looked at coldly, the death of the second Brandon heir no longer mattered; there would soon be another.

Beaulieu itself was unchanged outwardly, but within the once splendid place all was foreboding. Mistress Boleyn was married and crowned, despite the Pope's ban on the King's divorce; and the King in his turn accordingly disowned the Pope. It would not have been possible then to foresee all of the dolour that would drag on over the years; suffice it that at Beaulieu, the Princess at last was informed, and her readings aloud of Latin in her gruff Spanish voice grew hesitant; she no longer played her lute. Lady Salisbury was unchanged, but quiet and grave, spending much time at her prayers. Reginald Pole, who like a few others had made it clear to the King that he could not condone the Boleyn marriage, had fled abroad. It occurred to me for the first time that the prosperity of that family was being eaten away; Westhorpe itself, as I have said, had once belonged to the de la Poles, and we had visited it, the Countess and I, on our early progresses. She made fewer journeys now, keeping close about the Princess as though to solace her while she might. The girl's mother was neither permitted to visit her nor to send, and soon perhaps the Lady Governess would be removed also. Everything depended on the King's will, and on the child soon to be born to Mistress Boleyn, whom few could, then or later, call Queen Anne.

*   *   *

As the world knows, the child proved a girl. I saw nothing of the birth itself for the press of folk surrounding the great bed at Greenwich; it was hardly possible to breathe in the room, and I felt sympathy for the unseen woman in labour, who they said was narrow-hipped. Having ridden in behind Madge Douglas and the Princess, I stayed beyond the door and stared, first at the tapestry of the wise and foolish virgins on the further wall, which could be seen beyond the crowding heads, and then, from my outer shadows, at the Princess Mary herself. Her tiny figure was stiff as a wax image, her face set. She was sixteen years old, all her life reared mostly on strict texts and the Scriptures, not even permitted formerly to know of tales such as that of Sir Lancelot or the fairy Melusine. Now she was alone, avoided by those whose eye was fixed forever on their own advancement, and who therefore left her a little space in which to stand, withdrawing their garments. It was evident that the King's favour was no longer with his daughter. Madge Douglas, standing not far off, was differently placed; His Grace still called her his good niece Marg'et and made much of her, at least for the time. I felt that we were all of us standing on shifting sand. The inner room smelt of sweat, perfumes and humanity; the labouring woman's breaths sounded interminably through the hushed whispers as everyone waited for the child to be born. When it was, there was a lull, then more whispering. Presently I saw the wrapped bundle carried out at last, spidery fingers waving; I noticed them as I always notice others' hands. Presently the King came in, his great pink slab of a face above its golden beard not pleased. No doubt he felt foolish at having fathered another daughter, alive or not. They say it was the beginning of Mistress Anne's downfall, but that was rumoured only afterwards. We did not wait long about the chamber, but rode off, staying however in town for the christening.

4

I attended the new young Duchess of Suffolk for her first Court appearance, which was for that same christening of Mistress Anne's daughter she had borne the King. Kate wore her new matron's coif and it was strange to see her silky brown hair covered, but her eyes, bright as a robin's, were the same, surveying everything calmly. The red-headed baby, borne in at last by the old Duchess of Norfolk and clad in the long lace robe worn by all Queen Catharine's children and which with other things had been wrested from Her Grace lately at the favourite's command, was made a Christian soul. My father the Duke performed his part adequately as he did everything, holding the towel to catch the holy water as it dripped from the silver ewer on to the baby's head. She had been named Elizabeth for the King's dead mother. She would not be as beautiful, but the spidery fingers waved confidently as she was borne out. She had not cried with the water.

Still watching Kate—it was always a pleasure—I reflected that she was, after the old Norfolk Duchess whom nobody counted greatly, the first lady in the land after the Queen, whichever might be called so for the time. Today it was a triumph for the Norfolks, Anne Boleyn's kin. I had watched the old Duke incline his bitter head coldly over his great chain to acknowledge my father: they were natural enemies, the Howards having a more ancient name and a title on to which they had grimly hung since Bosworth and had retained after all because of Flodden. My father's quick rise to fortune despite the fact that Richard III, whom the Norfolk of that day had supported, had himself thrust his sword through the throat of my father's father—poor mother used to say that had he done it nine months earlier she would have been spared much shame—and the different tempers of the two men, made them fail to agree in any necessity save that of pleasing the King enough to keep their heads on their shoulders. Henry himself, beaming and expansive once more after the chagrin of the birth—at least a living child meant hope of more to come—came after the ceremony and cast his great arm in its purfled sleeve about my father's broad padded shoulders, they laughed together and then the Duke presented Kate. I saw the King's small eyes rove over her appreciatively; no doubt he would have liked her in his own bed. My Lady Salisbury, who in her time had carried Princess Mary to the font, remained in the shadows; I saw her incline her head in its long hood, but she did not speak to anyone. She maintained a place at Court to try to foster the cause of her charge the Princess, without evident hope meantime. I watched the gaudy changeable crowd about Court, made up mostly of brash new persons favoured by Mistress Anne, including Anne's brother who strode past noisily in the company of the King's bastard son Richmond, also himself married to a Howard. There had been whisperings that Richmond might be named heir to the throne instead of Princess Mary, even before this young new birth; but nothing was certain now. The King was calling himself Defender of the Faith, having forsworn the Pope but not the sacraments. A dark-jowled churchman named Cranmer had stood godfather to the baby in his lawn sleeves. My glance caught that of Lady Salisbury again, and I knew she was remembering that earlier and thankful christening of the child born after a long-ago prayer of the despairing Queen's at Walsingham.

* * *

We rode back to Beaulieu. Madge Douglas was of the party, though she had grown withdrawn and haughty and had stood at the christening twisting a ring on her finger which might have been Tom Howard's; it was whispered that they were secretly married although, because of Madge's nearness to the throne, it could not be openly permitted by the King until the new child was safely born. However seated with Madge later in the solar she revealed an inward calm happiness that only comes with love returned and given, and I envied her again for the time. She was working quietly—she was, surprisingly, a fine needlewoman—at a piece of lace made with a hairpin and a thread of her own long fine hair. She told me that she had passed many hours in this way in draughty Border castles such as Norham, where she had often waited for visits from her father during the high Tweed floods; he had always put her into shelter when he might. I watched the nimble fingers work the fine hair into a pattern of raised leaves; and thought how Queen Margaret's daughter had a strength of her own, as her pampered and faithless mother had not. She was talking now about the King's new decisions; they said already that, she, like the Princess, was stiff in her Poperies. So of course were the Norfolks, despite everything.

'I do not think that His Grace is right, but one cannot say as much anywhere but here,' Madge stated in her downright Scots fashion. 'Christ gave the keys to St Peter, not the King of England. I fear me there may be uprisings in the country when the news spreads, for the common folk will not welcome it, having no land to lose. They love Queen Catharine and her daughter, as do I.' She finished off the thread expertly and began to pull out another from beneath her hood. The Princess herself was not with us, but lying down on her bed meantime with one of her severe headaches: she did not enjoy good health since her separation from her mother. I stared down at my three-fingered hand and thought how much might come to pass even beyond England with this changing mind in the King. In King John's time there had been an interdict and much woe in England, but now there would be great offence abroad as well. The King of France might be a lecher, but he obeyed the Pope; so did the Emperor. 'The

King here once received the Pope's golden rose for making war against France,' murmured Madge, though it was not like her to look beyond near concerns. 'Should Christ's Vicar concern himself with wars?' I murmured, for this is the kind of untoward thought which sometimes afflicts me. I looked up then and saw Lady Salisbury standing quiet in the doorway, and knew that she had heard because she looked reproachful. She beckoned me to come and I did so, remarking on how empty the passages had lately grown beyond the unguarded rooms. The Princess Mary's household had once numbered one hundred and sixty persons, and now only a handful were left.

'Mag, dearest, mind your tongue,' said Lady Salisbury gently. 'It is not a time to talk so, even here. You are in any case to ride home at once; your father hath sent for you. Be sure to put on your warm cloak: it grows cold.'

I made my obeisance, kissed her long white hand, and sent my farewells to the Princess, hoping the latter would soon recover. Then I returned to say goodbye to Madge, who had risen at Lady Salisbury's entry and stood now with the half-finished hairpin work she had been at in her hand. She still had her look of calm inward contentment and seemed only half aware of coming change, being no doubt deep in love. A brief recollection of young Tom Howard flitted through my mind; he seemed a biddable enough young man and would suit Madge. The grey light from the window—the year was turning then—made her hair seem white for instants, an old woman's. Riding away with my father's escort that he had sent, I had the fancy that when Madge was old she might perhaps sit alone, making silver lace instead of gold, maybe in prison. There seemed no reason for this foreboding I had, except for the empty passages of Beaulieu and the sudden command of my father that I must return.

* * *

It had not immediately been made evident why I had been sent for again to Westhorpe, but it became clear soon that the house itself was full of trouble. The least of the matter was still poor Lincoln, coughing his way to death mostly upstairs with the consumption that had killed his mother in the summer. Downstairs, the hall was filled meantime with the strutting presence of little Dorset, Frances' husband, who like a cock-sparrow made a great deal of noise and boasting as if to offset his small size. Frances, his large hen, sat watching everyone, with neither illusion nor kindness in her hard grey eyes. There was no sign yet of a baby, and I wondered if Frances's Tudor appetites had been satisfied by her puny bridegroom, whose old mother the Marchioness in any case kept writing for money, which my father on the late magnificent marriage had promised to provide. I knew that the Duke was also in straits not only with the French dowry repayments to the King—Lady Willoughby sat by, as always keeping an eye to her daughter's inheritance, which would not be permitted to be squandered in such ways—but also with my troublesome half-sisters Powis and Mounteagle. Powis was already misbehaving herself at Court, using to the full the licence permitted by Anne Boleyn's easy following, for the marriage with my lord was not a happy one; his family had as I say made strict enquiries about Anne Brandon's legitimacy before permitting it, and only the evidence of her mother's miscarriage on receiving word of the pregnancy of my own had assured everyone that this Anne had been legally begotten after the public service of remarriage long ago at Stepney, and not before. As for Mary Monteagle, she and her husband were incurably spendthrift and I knew that my father, who was fond of his young daughter, often smuggled them jewels to sell. Altogether, although he romped and laughed with Kate as was his custom and could hardly keep his hands from her, it was clear that he was not himself; his big face had a preoccupied look it had not formerly worn in my recollection. It was Frances and none other who broke some of the news, though not yet all.

'You were brought home from Beaulieu in time, Mag,' she said to me spitefully; I never knew her to say a pleasant thing to anyone. 'There is no longer any establishment there; the place is empty, and the Lady Mary has been removed to Hunsdon in attendance on the new Princess.' She sounded smug; the affliction of others always gave her pleasure. I thought of the winter's wind blowing through empty Beaulieu, and asked coldly who the Lady Mary might be, although I knew. Frances bridled.

'With your experience of foreign Courts—' she had never forgiven me the years with Madame, for she herself would have loved to flaunt her hips at great occasions and had, on the contrary, in those early days been kept close at home in the country till the scandal over her prompt birth should have died down—'you should know that such matters are decided by the King's will. He has commanded that the Lady Mary his daughter be no longer known as Princess, as she is declared bastard, her mother having formerly been married to the King's own brother, as all knew. The Princess Elizabeth is present heir to the throne, but we must hope for brothers for her.'

So the Princess Mary, whom I myself would never call by any other name, was degraded to the position of a servant about her new half-sister, in a house which, I knew, either belonged to the Boleyn faction or else favoured them. 'What has become of my Lady Salisbury?' I asked lightly; one might as well learn as much from the opposing side as was possible without causing comment.

Frances shrugged her heavy shoulders above the square embellished neck of her gown. 'Why, that old woman has feathered her own nest from the beginning, and is back at Court; provided she minds her ways, no one will harm her.'

I kept my eyes down to hide my anger: it was probable that the Countess would continue to care for Princess Mary's interests at Court as much as it could now be done; quiet, unobtrusive, devout, her very presence would keep in His Grace's mind the dignified days of Queen Catharine and, no doubt, foster the interests of the Countess's own absent youngest son Reginald, at present with the Emperor; I knew this, for Lady Salisbury had secretly told me. It was not a thing to pass on. As if he had read my thoughts, Dorset strolled over to his wife.

'There will be trouble brewing for the old Princess Dowager now her daughter is disposed of,' he said. 'Together they were a threat to the reign: letters will no doubt have been sent abroad by them.' He spoke with a loud-voiced authority he did not possess; I doubted if he was in the King's confidence to any extent. Nevertheless it was as if a cold draught had trickled into the warm hall, like the changes coming in England. Queen Catharine was now the Princess Dowager; her daughter was no longer royal; the Pope was no longer supreme; and the King still had no son. All of it whirled in my head, and I rose from where I sat, leaving the Dorset couple together; they were as ill-assorted as the rest, except for my own father and young Kate, who seemed happy.

I went out into the cold garden, inclining my head as I passed to Lady Willoughby, who sat dark-eyed and watchful always in her place, saying little to anyone. I knew well enough that she was unchangingly loyal to Queen Catharine, and admired, though I did not greatly like her for herself, the way this Spanish widow continued to handle the difficulties here, in the heart of enmity, both for the imprisoned Queen's sake and for the weal of her own daughter, the new Duchess of Suffolk, third great lady of the land. That marriage had been a shrewd move. Nevertheless I was troubled for the Duke my father.

* * *

He came to me in the garden. It was cold, with the bare plots turned for coming frost to break up the waiting earth; the Queen-Duchess's knot-beds had been dug up, nobody now attending to them. My father stared at the place where they had been, no doubt remembering; then lowered his heavy-featured face into the fur collar of his coat, talking quietly: Dorset's loud voice still sounded from the house.

'Mag,' the Duke said, 'you are wise. There is no one else to whom I can speak at the moment; my wife is young, and governed by her mother still. I have waited to see you alone when I might do so without openly sending for you; we are watched always, even now.' His small eyes glanced sideways uneasily in his great face, still flushed with the late heat from the hall.

'What have you to fear?' I said, a trifle unwillingly; I too was remembering the Queen-Duchess, the royal wife who had so greatly loved Charles Brandon, to whom it would have been safe enough for him to speak: and whose body lay now in the Abbey beneath layers of gold cloth. 'You have the King's favour,' I added. I said no more on that; he had weathered the storm of the French marriage, and had made another profitably and soon. He spread out his hands then in a little helpless gesture, strange from so big a strong man.

'I remain in His Grace's favour by carrying out his commands,' he said, 'and he knows it, and so does Secretary Cromwell. Lately the orders sent by letter trouble me more than I can say. I have been making preparations these last few days to do what I must; but I do it unwillingly, between fear of the King if I do not, and fear of the Emperor if I do. You are the Emperor's friend: if it must be, Mag, speak for me. It is possible Charles V will even make war on England for his aunt's sake, and for that of the Princess to whom he was once betrothed. He will also remember that I myself was said to presume—' he smiled—'to intend to marry his aunt, Madame of the Netherlands.' He related again the tale of the ring and the King's ill-timed jest at Térouenne. 'I do not think that she was indifferent to me, although I was a man who had risen from nothing and she a princess of most ancient blood and name,' he said. It was part of the reason why so many women loved my father, and no doubt the King also, that he could speak so, as if it concerned another than himself. It came to me that I loved him greatly and had begun to do so at my first coming home out of Flanders.

'What is this command of the King's that so greatly troubles you?' I asked my father. I knew he had been putting off relating it, as men and small boys will for as long as they can. However it had best come out now, while we were still undisturbed; others would have seen us walking in the garden, and the Duke's company was forever sought.

His voice came then unsteadily. 'I could not tell you myself, Mag, of the breaking up of

Beaulieu,' he said. 'The Lady Mary herself, young as she is, by stratagems put that off as long as she might. Now that it is done, and she herself under watchful eyes at Hunsdon, I am—' he lowered his head and mumbled, as if in confession—'I am commanded to go to Buckden, where the—the Princess Dowager is, and take her under guard to Somersham, where she will be kept close prisoner. It is an unhealthy place. There is no doubt that His Grace hopes she will die there. I have compassion for the woman: good God, I remember how she tugged at His Grace's surcoat to get him away from wrestling with King Francis when they met together at the Field of the Cloth of Gold! She and Queen Claude pulled the two great men apart, fearing they would do themselves an injury although it was supposedly in jest: but they were rivals. Queen Catharine had always an eye to her husband; she loved him. Nor do I like injuring any woman so; and she is a good woman, though stubborn, and barren by now, as all know.'

No, you do not like hurting women, I thought, and so you have done harm to many by obliging them; but this act would be intentional, yet one he could not refuse to carry out. 'The King forgave me much when I married his sister, and took away a bride from the Emperor thereby,' I heard the Duke say. 'Truth to tell I never saw a woman so weep, and so I told the King; who could have resisted her as she was then? She had loved me long, and said His Grace had promised that if she married old King Louis she should have her own choice next time if he should die. Then they wanted her for the Emperor, and King Francis wanted her for himself; and I took her from them all, and am maybe not forgiven.'

'There was love between the pair of you,' I said. 'You were most happy together.'

'I do not forget,' my father said simply. Then he started murmuring about the dowry repayments, and how there was a possibility that the King would waive these if the Duke himself now carried out this unpleasant latest bidding. 'I dare not fail him,' my father said. 'I have men-at-arms ready to ride. We leave tomorrow.'

Men-at-arms, ready to dislodge a helpless woman separated from her daughter; it was true that the Emperor might be angry when he heard. 'Have no fear,' I said suddenly, knowing my father's lack of choice in the matter. 'The Emperor is my friend, as you say, because of a thing I once said to him in Flanders. I will do what I may, being myself of no importance: nobody will heed me, or whether or not I write.'

He went away then, a little comforted, and next day in the chapel took Communion, kneeling with bared head and his basnet ready in his hand to put on his head and ride; and presently they all rode out, making a great clatter of lances and armour, to remove the Princess Dowager forcibly to Somersham. I saw Lady Willoughby watch them go, and knew that she knew why. She had her informers, as I had mine; but as we did not trust one another our speech was of other things when we spoke at all.

Meantime I remembered why the Emperor continued my friend, and knew how I could perhaps reach him; through Lady Salisbury's absent son, Reginald Pole. I could see my lady less safely at Court than at the Charterhouse vespers, where she often went; many still did, even in these days when the famous house was watched for its constant allegiance and denial of the King's supremacy as head of the Church. The Prior, John Houghton, had by then I believe taken a modified oath, but a firmer one was to be demanded which he refused, with heroic constancy.

* * *

After my father and his men had ridden off I excused myself to the rest and went upstairs alone to my attic room. I took my writing-things and wrote a letter at once, hiding it in my bodice, when it was dry, intending to keep it there safe until the Dorsets should have left the house. There might not be an opportunity to write again, for I knew we would be in town all together at least for Twelfth-night; and later, after the hot weather had made London unsuitable, at one or other of little Kate's houses, no doubt Tattershall, a tall tower in the midst of flat country where one could ride daily. It was probable, though nobody had said it, that Westhorpe would soon be in other hands. We must move on, as Lady Salisbury had had to do from there in her time; perhaps her quiet ghost and the Queen-Duchess's would one day walk together in what had been the knot-garden.

* * *

My letter was in Latin, and began *Imperator*. This was the code-name with which both his aunt Madame and I myself, and others who knew him well, had been used to address Charles V, Holy Roman Emperor, King of Spain, and own nephew to the Queen of England. As for the language, all tongues had been chattered freely at Madame's Flemish Court; they said the Emperor himself talked French to his enemies, German to his friends, Spanish to his women, and Italian to his horse. His English was not good, although he had once hunted with my father at Southwark in the days when he had briefly visited England as the young Princess's betrothed. I reminded him of that; and my letter read towards its end

Do not blame my father for what he must

now do; he is cruelly placed and has no choice but to obey. You know that I am always your devoted servant and friend, as we vowed that day before the portrait of the Queen of Castile, your mother. I signed myself MM. If the letter fell into the wrong hands, I reflected wryly that they might well blame Mary Mounteagle for it; she had after all been in Flanders at the same time as the episode I now remembered.

* * *

It had happened in Madame's rich Flemish palace of Lille, shortly after I myself had come over from England. I was unhappy, being kindly treated by neither of my half-sisters and not yet under the full notice of Madame. I had stood alone while the others danced to the boisterous Flemish musicians, myself staring meantime at a pair of portraits on the wall. One was of a sullen young man in armour, seen in profile, a helmet on his head. This was Philip the Handsome, Madame's only brother, and that likeness did not do him justice; I have seen better renderings of him, one on a tapestry in Spain of which he was briefly king. He was dead long since, it was said of poison by King Ferdinand, but that is always whispered when a ruler dies young. Beside the portrait was another, of a young woman with long dark hair combed loose, and a face so beautiful it was like that of the Mother of God.

She wore a bright cloak of many colours which did not conceal her body, which was far gone with child, that last being perhaps the Emperor himself. It was his mother Juana, Philip's wife, by right Queen of Castile, but imprisoned by her own father Ferdinand with rumours spread that she was mad. The world had long been sustained on this rumour. Queen Juana was still in prison in a fortress near the Portuguese border; it suited nobody to set her free, and they said she was even kept in a room without windows so that she could not look out of them and call for help. She had been there now many years.

I became aware of being watched, and turned to behold a grave young man with a pale face and a strangely protruding lower jaw. It was the Emperor, and I sank in my deepest obeisance, then rose as he smiled a little. His mouth was so awkwardly kept open always that when he had ridden first through Spain, his mother's inheritance, they had called out after him that he could catch flies in it. I knew that he had seen my own deformity, and suddenly spoke to him as if he had been anyone, which few did. I knew what to say.

'Your mother was so beautiful,' I told him, 'that when she and your father were shipwrecked and visited the Court at Windsor, the King, Henry VII, never forgot her. After his queen died, and your father was dead also, he wanted to marry Queen Juana himself. It did not matter to him what they said. He was a cautious man, but that time he forgot his caution. He never forgot your mother.' Lady Salisbury, who had been present as a girl, had told me of that. I smiled, and for the first time easily, for I was still shy, looked steadily at the Emperor with my unequal eyes. He had after all his strange outlandish jaw; we all have our crosses. He replied courteously and said he remembered his father well, and had been brought up to revere his memory by Madame after his death. I said nothing of what I knew, which was that Philip the Handsome had been treacherous and unfaithful. I knew Charles V could seldom have heard his mother spoken of favourably and that he was glad of what I had told him. Thereafter we were friends, inasmuch as a lone young woman can be said to be so with a great ruler unless she is his mistress. He had one then, a young Fleming who bore him a daughter. Later, when he married Isabel of Portugal, he was a loving husband to her although he had to be often absent, and they called their two children Philip and Juana. Juana like her grandmother was very beautiful, but so pious the world has hardly heard of her. The Emperor took his children more than once to visit his mother in her prison at Tordesillas, but never let her reign. By then, it would have been impossible. Charles V had so great an inheritance, half the world, that it was almost too great a burden for one man. It could never have been done by a woman, even Charles's militant and, to my mind, ruthless grandmother Isabella of Castile, who had driven the Moors out of Spain.

* * *

The attempt to remove Queen Catharine by force from Buckden failed: my father rode home two days later grim-mouthed, and still in his basnet and leather jack strode into his study to dictate letters to Master Secretary Cromwell and the King. Afterwards he came up to us in the solar; none of us had dared ask one another what had happened. We had been seated, till the Duke came, sewing young Eleanor's bride-clothes; she was soon to be married to Lord Clifford, the Earl of Cumberland's son. I remember raising my head often from the sewing, at which my poor hand was not apt, and gazing at a lute which lay there silent, its ribbons stirring faintly with the draught from the brazier. Beyond the room it was very cold. We could hear the Duke's voice downstairs, growing louder as he ascended.

He came in presently and kissed Kate; I could tell that he was drunk with wine. This was seldom the case, as he demeaned himself as a rule with propriety not only before his young wife, but before her mother, who was still with us for the season. It was evident, therefore, that some matter at Buckden must have unmanned my father; and what it was became evident. He, an armed man in full charge of a party of horse, together with the Earl of Sussex and his, not to mention the Dean of the Chapel Royal as well to lend the King's authority, had none of them reckoned with the force of the Queen's Spanish will. The woman who had won Flodden, the daughter of soldier Isabella, was now besieged on her own account, and showed an equal courage to her mother's. I glanced at Lady Willoughby as the tale proceeded, wondering if she also thought of Castile and their youth; but she kept her eyes down, listening and sewing on.

'I would not have credited it,' said my father thickly, his arm about Kate. 'She—I did not see her, none did, for she would not come out, behaving like an animal in a burrow. They say her food is cooked in the room where she sleeps, for fear of poison. She shouted at us through a hole in the wall that she would not come with us, that she refused to dress herself, that she would go to bed and stay there so that we could not move her. The servants, most of 'em, refused likewise to obey the King, and swear allegiance to the woman as Princess Dowager, the widow of his brother Arthur and no more. They said they had already done so to her as Queen, and Queen she was to them still, and they were advised by those two fools of chaplains of hers that they would perjure themselves by altering an oath already taken. Churchmen! They do more harm than all the rest. I left that damned Spanish confessor of hers with her, as he's harmless; and locked the other two in the gatehouse.' The Duke's great wine-flushed face looked round at us all defiantly.

'So she will not go to Somersham,' said Lady Willoughby, not as though she was surprised. 'That is an unhealthy place, not that Buckden is much better, being damp and half ruinous.' She spoke without emotion, but I saw fierce hatred flash for a moment in her eyes before they lowered themselves again. It had occurred to me to wonder what Maria Willoughby felt at news of the treatment of her beloved friend and mistress, at the same time as having arranged an advantageous match for her daughter with that very friend's foe, or at least with a man held high in the counsels of the King. My father noticed nothing, merely replying sullenly, 'She will not, as I've said. Nor will she obey other of the King's decrees, saying she is still his wife although she will bear no son. The common folk were all about the doors, weeping and praying for her. There would have been rioting to quell if we'd stayed; in the end there was naught to do but go, all of us, like fools, troops and horse.' He fondled his wife. 'Kate, little Kate, you are all my comfort! Do not you turn to a stubborn mule of a woman when you're grown, sweetheart; be you my dove and liking, as always.' His fondlings grew more intimate, as if the rest of us had not been present; his great face was scarlet with wine. Kate played as she often did with his beard, which had turned white. She was smiling. I heard poor young Lincoln, dying by then, cough upstairs where he lay sadly alone. The rest of us got on with our sewing by the light of candles, as the Clifford wedding was drawing near, while the Duke departed with Kate to bed. That night, I am certain, he got her with child. It was by then near Christmas.

*　　*　　*

I had never greatly liked Lady Willoughby, whom I thought hard and harsh-voiced, but there is no doubt that, even before the matter of the Queen's dying, she proved herself a valiant woman. She came and went, keeping an eye on Kate as the latter's time drew near, and before that continuing her running battle with the Willoughby kinsman over Grimsthorpe and the other properties due to Kate which were in dispute; in the end, she won. Also, she was with us for poor Lincoln's funeral when it occurred. Meantime the Queen, to be put out of reach of the common folk, was removed in the end, not to Somersham but to Kimbolton, perhaps being by then too ill to resist further; it was said she had a constant clutching pain about her heart. That last had been greatly tried. By the time—it was a year later, in January—that she was known at last to be sick unto death, none were still allowed near her but her guards, nor, though Queen Catharine begged for it, was she allowed to see her daughter even for the last time of all. Despite all his cruelties Catharine of Aragon still loved the King; perhaps she thought of him as the handsome boy she had married long ago who had rescued her from poverty and neglect, and had fathered her dead children and her living child. *Mine eyes desire to behold you above all things.* The Duke was with His Grace when that letter came, but the King's face revealed nothing, nor did he go to Kimbolton. Maria Willoughby did, and by a ruse; riding hard with her train along the rutted frozen roads, she fell from her horse of set purpose, risking her limbs, near the place itself, and staggered bruised and mud-stained to the outer door, being told at first that none might enter, as that was the King's order. Lady Willoughby declared that she was half-fainting, and asked to be allowed at least to warm herself before their fire in the hall, saying then that she would show them a signed pass when she could obtain her baggage to open it. They let her in, and once in nothing would keep her from the stairs, and upstairs the Queen herself lay dying; and having run up and gained the chamber at last my lady put her arms about her to cheer her, and nothing could make her leave till the Queen was dead. I may say here that after her own death, which happened only a few years afterwards, Maria Willoughby asked to be buried at her mistress's feet at Peterborough, and this was done. However before then, many other things had happened, both in my own life and in the state of affairs in England.

* * *

Anne Boleyn had of course dressed in yellow, to show her joy, at the Queen's death; and had made His Grace do likewise, saying that now she was truly queen. By then she was however certainly falling out of favour, being grown too free and bold in her manners: and bore a dead boy soon, it was said from dismay at finding the King with prim quiet Jane Seymour perched on his knee.

* * *

By then, the young Duchess of Suffolk my stepmother, aged fifteen, had borne her own first son safely, at the Barbican house in mid-September of 1534. I have never seen a more delightful baby, strong and lively with a puckish face and bright hair. My father came in with his heavy handsome countenance beaming with relief and pride, and kissed Kate tenderly. There was certainly affection between them; the marriage was happy. Kate sighed to me that she was not a cobbler's wife, and might then have fed her baby herself; but he was carried off to the wet-nurse, and called after the King. I marvelled at the benign fate that always seemed to follow my father Charles Brandon, squire of many dames, among them royal Mary and Madame of the Netherlands, and now Kate, heiress of great acres.

He wrote, with the news of his son's safe arrival, to Master Secretary Cromwell, who had much influence with the King in those days. I disliked the man's grey pig-eyed face, but then I disliked the King's pink one. Meantime, I played with the baby, never expecting to have one of my own; young Harry Lincoln was enchanting, and grew daily, being forward and strong.

* * *

There was a crooked elm in the Prior's Charterhouse garden, so old that its boled trunk lay along the grass, with February snowdrops thrusting their way up through. The weather was not too cold for the time of year. I walked with Lady Salisbury, having slipped in to meet her, as I often did, from the Barbican house nearby. She had already, on a previous such encounter, taken my letter to the Emperor to send by way of her son. We talked in hushed voices now in order not to disturb the Carthusian brothers' quiet; time had been when they desired to know nothing that went on in the world beyond, but these days it was increasingly hard not to do so. Humphrey Middlemore, the procurator, had of necessity to go into the city to buy provisions, and could not help but hear what concerned them all.

He came hurrying towards us now across the grass like an oversized magpie, his black cloak flying back to reveal his white Carthusian robe. His face was troubled, as it had not formerly been; there were new lines on it.

'My lady, my lady! Remember us in your good prayers! There is great trouble.' He spoke in a low voice. 'You will recall that the Prior and I myself were conveyed to the Tower last May, to take the oath regarding the King's new marriage. He took it, as the clauses left room for conscience then; but even so, many here blamed him. Now, there is an edict given out that to deny the King's title of Supreme Head of the Church in England is treason. Prior Houghton will not subscribe.'

'Christ gave the keys to St Peter,' said my lady calmly. The Procurator spread out his hands.

'That is God's truth, which none can deny; so how can we take the oath? Ever since the summer there has been dissension here among us, with some of the less steady brethren seeing, or fancying they see, portents everywhere of disaster; a comet, swarms of flies, a flock of crows attacking the Prior's habit as it hung on the washing line; that last happened, but the rest—' Humphrey Middlemore shook his head; it was a scholar's, for he had read at Cambridge, like many of the monks, before entering the Order. He was not a young man.

'Nothing can separate us from the love of Christ,' said Lady Salisbury. 'I have reason to know that well, through many trials. I will pray, as you ask.'

'We have all prayed to God,' said the Procurator. 'These last three days have been set aside for particular prayer and confession among us, one to another. This is the third day, and Prior Houghton will say Mass, beseeching the Holy Spirit to come to us in our trials.'

'God will not deny you. We will attend the Mass if we may.' She turned and looked at me, and I nodded; Kate and my father would wonder where I was, but it mattered nothing. Again I saw Lady Salisbury's eyes shine like jewels, clear with certainty and faith; her very presence seemed to calm the poor Procurator. At the same time we saw three figures approach at the further end of the garden, and pass by saluting gravely; Prior Houghton himself, a stern man of great dignity, and two visitors, both monks, who had come for advice on the matter from outlying monasteries. We did not disturb their silence, but when they had gone inside the Countess spoke again.

'Nothing will have any effect on the King's Grace but a calamity or something that makes him afraid. So says my son Reginald.' She pronounced it Reynald, as always. 'He knows the King as well as any man; he was his scholar and close to him. Nobody was more greatly amazed than Reginald himself when, that time before he left England, asked by the King regarding the marriage, God told him to make a different answer from the one he had fully intended to make. My son made it with tears, but the truth was put in his mouth. I do not think the King will forgive him for it; thankfully, he is abroad. He saw the Pope lately in Rome, and was greatly comforted.'

I did not ask about my letter to the Emperor; it no longer mattered. We went into the chapel in due course, and knelt before the exposed Host. Several were there already from the Court; increasingly, as minds grew troubled, many came who had not come before to the House of the Salutation of the Mother of God, formerly a place of peace. The bell rang and I saw the monks file in, and knew one face among them; Sebastian Newdigate, a young man who had been a favourite about Court, but had given up the world as Chancellor More had tried to do, himself having served here in the Charterhouse for four years before leaving it, having decided after all that his life was in the world. He was now in the Tower, having displeased the King by like reason of conscience.

The Prior had vested, and began to say Mass. His voice was true and deep; John Houghton loved good music and correct chanting. He was hard on his novices, and was said to have walked out of church often enough if somebody sang a false note, reprimanding them afterwards. Nevertheless the brothers loved him, though there had been dissension among them, as Middlemore had said, by reason of the Prior's acceptance of the first form of oath; but he would certainly not accept this second form. What would happen next was clear; I knew John Houghton knew he was doomed, and that all did likewise. His face at first had had a set look, but at the Elevation a strange thing happened: I was not alone in sensing this. A whispering as light as air, a most lovely sound, like the voice of a gentle breeze, the voice Elijah heard with his face wrapped in his cloak, passed from one end of the chapel to the other. It was the Holy Ghost. Prior Houghton dissolved in tears; he was unable to continue the Mass for some time. Then he finished: we received Communion, the Countess and I, having both confessed lately. With the taking of the bread I had the feeling that I was in the close presence of martyrs. Had I known, there was one also beside me.

* * *

Within a few days the Prior was taken once more, and tried at Westminster with the two others we had seen who had come to seek his advice, and bravely took this. I did not see for myself what happened then, but heard of it with the rest of England. Five days after the trial Houghton and his Carthusians, all three in their white habits, with a Bridgettine monk from Syon and John Hale the parish priest from Isleworth who had refused the oath, were dragged on hurdles to Tyburn and there hanged, drawn and quartered. Afterwards the dead Prior's arm was nailed by the King's order over Charterhouse gate. Thomas More, late Chancellor, had watched from his prison window as the hurdles passed by. His own martyrdom, for the same cause, would not be long in coming.

* * *

I was disturbed at something young Kate said about then. It showed she had little sympathy with the Catholic martyrs and no doubt favoured the King, who in turn favoured her as she always pleased him. It was not yet possible for so young a girl to use her mind extensively on such matters, as Kate did later. The new thought, as they called it—there had been outbursts of new thought since the time of all heresies—was slow in forming itself, and the Henrician Church, as they began to name it, for a time resembled the old closely enough for few to question the difference, and many of those few to lose their heads accordingly. Meantime a certain cleric, who was greatly to influence Duchess Kate, came to the house as chaplain, which he had formerly been to Anne Boleyn; she had had him made a bishop but he cared nothing for that. His name was Hugh Latimer. He was always dressed plainly, in an old black woollen gown with spectacles pinned to it. He had a ready apt tongue and an earthy wit which suited Kate, but I did not like him, and kept my own silence. I do not know what my father thought; he let Kate do as she would in such matters. She herself would discourse with this Latimer by the hour, playing often with her baby whom she had had brought downstairs. She was still so near childhood herself that the new Earl of Lincoln might have been her mammet: she took great delight in him. He was still the handsomest child I have ever seen.

* * *

The King's self-will increased to monstrosity in that blood-soaked year of 1535. Whoever crossed it suffered, more perhaps if His Grace had formerly loved them; such a one was Thomas More, who lost his head that summer, but it was a clean death at the least. After him died Bishop Fisher, so saintly an old man that his very flesh was wasted to the bone with penance and mortification; this could be seen after the naked headless body, stripped by the executioner, lay on the scaffold for the summer flies to swarm in its congealing blood. A common man, brave enough to defy the King's wrath, climbed up and covered the private parts with straw as soon as he might safely do so after the crowds had gone: the body stayed thus till they took it away. The Pope had sent John Fisher a cardinal's hat lately: 'I will leave him no head to put it on,' had remarked the King. Many heads were to fall, not least that of Mistress Anne herself in the following year, but she also died quickly with a single stroke of the sword brought purposely over from Calais. The King then married his Jane, and declared both his daughters bastard.

I myself had already gone back at times to the Charterhouse, though Lady Salisbury being away by then on her estates I was no longer admitted to the Prior's garden. Differences showed sadly in the outer cloister, where traders by now peddled their wares and royal commissioners came and went noisily; they visited the monks in their cells to disturb them, and harangued loudly even at Mass, which was often prevented. Bereft of their Prior, the brothers resisted stoutly for a time, refusing to read the anti-papal sheets Cromwell forced on them and seeing, a month after John Houghton's arm had been nailed above the gate, three more, Middlemore the procurator among them, taken away to prison, chained there by the neck and legs for two weeks, then tried and executed like the others. Among them was young Brother Sebastian Newdigate, former darling of the Court. Still others of the Carthusians were taken and forced to listen to a hostile sermon at Paul's Cross, exposed to the gaze of the crowding curious people; they behaved with dignity and took no notice, but inside the monastery they were being deprived of food. Nothing was left undone to break their resistance, even to lies told abroad to the Grand Prior of their order, who sent the beleaguered house a remonstrance for disobeying the Crown.

There was all of this; but the thing I remember most clearly, for I saw it for myself at Smithfield, was the burning of the friar John Forrest, who had been Queen Catharine's confessor and like the others refused to deny the Pope. He was roasted slowly in an iron cradle over a slow fire, and jeering steadily above him was none other than Hugh Latimer, giving vent to one of his earthy humorous sermons as the friar writhed in agony, not by any means dying quickly. I loathed Latimer thereafter and could hardly bear to be in the same room with him when he came to the Duchess as usual; I would make some excuse and go out. I felt only triumph when he in his turn was burned, twenty years after, in a ditch at Oxford when Mary Tudor became queen. Latimer's own burning at least was swift.

* * *

They say the old must go to the wall. This simply means that in former courteous times, a bench was reserved for their use against it. I was thirty-one years old. I sat on one such in what had been the convent of Holywell until the King had given it last year to Lord Rutland. In the way of other such places it had then been shorn of holy objects and made into a house for my lord and his family to live in; many of the former nuns had been forced accordingly to beg on the roads, for only the larger convents were still permitted to remain in existence, and they were full. Nevertheless there was a wedding in progress here today, with a Mass already said for three brides, one of them by now my Lady Nevill and my kinswoman, for which reason I myself had been bidden.

The Mass over, there was to be dancing, but I knew no man would want to hold my crippled hand. I kept it in my sleeve, recalling again how poor Anne Boleyn in her time had designed wide falling ones to hide her sixth finger. I had the strong feeling that Anne's ghost was present, though there seemed no reason.

Her death had brought troubles to certain ones still left alive; Madge Douglas, now suddenly too near the throne now the King's two daughters were declared bastard, had been clapped in the Tower, separately from Tom Howard, who was in there likewise. A marriage, even a reputed one, with the Norfolk clan would not be admissible, even though Anne Boleyn's own uncle Norfolk had presided at her trial. It was rumoured that the Queen of Scots, Madge's hitherto neglectful mother, had at last written to the King her brother to demand her daughter back, hearing of her late imprisonment: but Madge would not want to return to the north, and to her mother's succession of husbands, which to date numbered the same as her brother the King's wives, to wit three, the last a young man. She was reputed to be desirous now of leaving this third and returning to the second, Madge's father the Earl of Angus; but at the time of her separation from him had openly declared that her first, James IV, was reputed to be still alive, a pilgrim to Jerusalem, not dead at Flodden as was supposed. Queen Margaret's claims were no longer taken seriously by anyone; she was an unprincipled woman and, unlike her royal brother, a fool.

He himself strode in presently among the throng of dancing folk, disguised as a Turk with a visor, and white feathers pinned in his black velvet turban. It was impossible not to know him because of his great height and breadth, and the ability he had to fill any hall with his presence. Everyone pretended not to know who he was, and he mingled with the dancers expertly, being light on his feet like many big men. I saw him partner little Kate, who danced heartily again now that she had borne her second son safely last spring. They laughed together, her small hand clasped in his large one and leaping in the figures lustily; I saw the King's eyes gleam below the visor, but he was happy enough meantime with his Jane. The music thumped on and I thought of the King's absent son Richmond, who had been expected here today but had sent word he was not well. The King did not appear troubled; perhaps the illness was nothing, or else perhaps Queen Jane was pregnant. Frances Dorset was said to be so, at last, after three years, by her mean bullying little husband; her belly, whether this was true or not, bounced as it always had. Later the King's visor was whipped off and amazement was pretended at the sight of the big solid small-eyed face, flushed with exertion and heat. The music stopped and we were all led to the banquet, my own place being set far from the high table;

I was used to this, being on sufferance as a Nevill now my mother was dead and no longer an embarrassment. The three brides, Ladies Bulbeck, Nevill and Roos, giggled and spooned their syllabubs at last, while the three grooms quaffed their wine meaningfully. There would be heirs made this night to ancient houses, as well as to some less ancient: as many new nobles were being made now as in the time of the King's father, and rewarded with filched Church lands for their service. Beggars thronged the roads with the closing of the monasteries, having no one any more to house them overnight or to heal their sores; it was said they were to be made a charge on the parishes shortly. I felt like a sibyl, a death's head at the feast; I was still aware of the presence of Anne Boleyn, standing now by the King's shoulder. I tried to listen to the chatter of the woman seated next me, and stop pretending to see what in truth I could not; but the certainty remained that Anne was there. I crumbled my bread and the woman stared at my hand, her mouth fallen open. I do not remember of what we talked before or after.

The hall had grown unbearably hot, and the King rose to leave before the bridal six were bedded. The remains of forty dishes lay strewn about the tables, and we heard the train of riders clatter off back to York Place, still in their black and purple Turkish robes, snowy feathers blown against black velvet in the early

June night.

A few days later the King's son Richmond, got long ago on Bess Blount, was dead. They said His Grace inveighed bitterly against his late Queen Anne, blaming her sorceries. I suppose it was in truth the same wasting disease that had carried off the Queen-Duchess and her two sons, and Prince Arthur of Wales the King's elder brother before that; sickly Tudor plants, all of them, that had not taken strong root. Nevertheless I cannot forget the feeling that Anne Boleyn had herself come to the feasting, and stood behind the King's shoulder to take away his son. I told no one of it but Tom Blakeborn, later: but by then I told Tom everything.

* * *

Shortly it was reported that the Queen went about with her placket unlaced. It seemed as if the King might have made another son to replace Richmond, and, they said, kept patting her belly and murmuring, 'Edward, Edward.'

5

Others besides myself—except perhaps Cardinal Wolsey in his time, to whom the Duke had spoken brutally to please the King—had had occasion to remark my father's kindness and good-nature. These were the qualities that had no doubt endeared him to all his women, including his young wife Kate; also perhaps His Grace himself, who was beginning to demand the title of Majesty instead. As for the Duke's children, including myself, we had seldom asked him for anything in vain, not that I asked for much: Powis and Mounteagle took extreme advantage of him, however, their loose behaviour being by now the talk of the Court, for the new Queen was strait-laced. Even a daughter of my mother's by her first marriage to Sir John Mortymer had appealed to the Duke in some dispute or other, and he had done his best for her also.

Of the two daughters the King's sister Mary had borne my father, I liked Frances Dorset least, and her husband less as I have often said. The Cliffords, married now two years, were a different matter, though I had no illusions about Eleanor's deceit and pretensions. No doubt it was partly that she had always been overridden by Frances in their childhood, and now desired to assert herself by insistence on the same royal pedigree. Poor Clifford suffered, and his father the Earl, in their pockets; Eleanor had grown so grand that she demanded much ceremony, and it had been necessary to rebuild a great new wing of Skipton Castle before it could be considered fit to receive her. All this cost more money than Cumberland could find, and when matters came down to the ground at last Eleanor herself found that she was short of that, but was not prepared to admit as much either to her husband, or to her two sisters-in-law whom she often visited at Bolton. From there she wrote to my father, somewhat deviously. If he would advance her a named sum of money meantime, a trustworthy man would receive it at the inn called the Old Man and Scythe at Bradshawgate, in order that none might know openly of the loan. The Duke laughed in his beard at this letter, having sent for me.

'You had best ride north, Mag,' he said. 'Nobody will suspect you of carrying silver to the great lady of Skipton.' This was before the uprising in Lincolnshire, as otherwise the Duke would not have sent me into danger.

I set out, therefore, with a small band of armed attendants out of livery, and journeyed on till the nature of the land began to change from our green flats to high unknown moors, with hills swelling in the distance rough and brown, and shaped like women's breasts. The roads were dry and we made timely going, at last clattering up the Bradshawgate towards the ancient inn. I sent a man off to the castle to let great Eleanor know that her trusty fellow might come when he would. As there was at present no sign of him, I sat down and ate my dinner.

Presently, as I was finishing, my father's man returned, and behind him a short broad-shouldered figure with shrewd and kindly hazel eyes. He might have been forty years of age. I felt myself rise to my feet; I was certain we had met before, and knew then, even so soon, that we had been destined to meet again. I can say no more of it than that, and that he felt it also, and later told me as much.

'I remember you,' he said quietly, 'from the court of Flanders. I have seen you often stand and read Latin quatrains aloud to Madame. Your voice is most beautiful.'

His name was Tom Blakeborn. I cannot remember that first meeting together we had again without deep emotion. It was thereafter as though there were only the two of us in all the world.

*   *   *

Next day I walked the little distance to St Peter's church and gave thanks, kneeling on the floor. It was one of those places not yet despoilcd. Humbly and before the Host, I recalled the things Tom had told me as we talked to one another far into the night; how he himself had been trained as a priest, but at the last moment, at the very ordination, had turned back. 'I knew the theology, the dialectic, the Latin chants, all of them,' he had said. 'I greatly desired to serve God, and had thought that must be the way; yet was told, in the end, after all that it was not. That happens to some.' The brilliant eyes regarded me from above a long neck. He had a beautiful face, not fashioned in the way of ordinary men's; small ears, a strong questing nose, a sensitively modelled mouth and a long jaw like an angel's, full of good and determined will, with a cleft chin. He had laughed at his bodily failings as he held my crippled hand; he was bald, he said, and had bent leg-bones below the knee, otherwise would have been a tall man. 'It has always troubled me till now, but now nothing does any more.' He asked me then to marry him.

'Why did you not ask me in Flanders?' I said, my hand still in his; the warmth of his grasp gave me strength. 'We have lost seven years.'

'I was not certain of myself; I, a failed priest, and you the favoured companion of Madame herself, in any case taken away to England before I dared speak. Now, with her death, I am in the service of her nephew the Emperor. Nobody knows this but yourself.' He added that Charles V was deeply concerned with the fate of the Princess Mary, who as all Catholics did he considered still to be the true heir to the throne of England, the King's marriage to Jane Seymour not having taken place with the approval of the Pope. 'I am to report to him constantly what befalls in England; I have a pass to come and go as a Flemish merchant, among other guises.' He told me his mother had been Flemish, his father an Englishman. 'At times, if you see me, you must not know me; at others, I must leave you for the time and you must not ask why, or try to follow. Knowing all this, if you will be my wife it will be the greatest happiness.' His voice faltered and we kissed each other. It was as though we were already one flesh.

'I will ask nothing,' I said. 'I will know nothing, except what you tell me, and that I will keep to myself. In any case I talk to few.' I remembered chattering Eleanor, bullying Frances, wanton Mounteagle and Powis and the rest as if they were phantoms in a different world, beyond a curtain. This new world was real. It did not matter who Tom was, or who he had been or might in future become. I loved him, and wondrously, amazingly, he loved me.

* * *

We were married, and I wrote to my father. It

had not been necessary to ask any one's permission or consent; I was of age and my own mistress, with a little money inherited from my mother, dead some years since by then. When the priest had done marrying us and we had exchanged rings, Tom again took hold of my crippled hand: it was almost as if it had grown a new finger and a thumb. I had parted with him briefly already in order that he might deliver the money to the Lady Eleanor, found seated gossiping as expected with her Cumberland sisters-in-law; she had asked idly where I was, but had not waited for any answer. 'They were talking of a thing that has happened here,' Tom said afterwards. 'Sir William Askew, a local landowner, had a young daughter married at fifteen to a man named Kyme, very proud of his name. There were children of the marriage, but Kyme has lately turned her out of doors for proclaiming the Gospel about the streets, saying she should have been looking after her house and the children. She has made her way to London to sue for a separation, preaching all the way on the roads.'

I smiled, and meantime forgot Anne Askew. We had stayed on at the inn for a few days, troubled by nobody; and one morning rode up with bread and cold meat and a flask of ale on to the moors, packing the food in our saddle-bags. We dismounted and sat down and ate among the heather, and Tom told me more of what it had not been safe to say aloud in the town's streets, let alone the inn, where even French or Spanish might have been understood. He spoke again of the Emperor.

'He would once have been married to the Princess Mary himself, as you know, but events at that time in England made her position uncertain,' he said. 'Now he thinks of her either for his brother Ferdinand, or else his son Philip, who is however still young.'

I reminded him that the King's son Prince Edward by then lived, and was said by all to be a fine child, and healthy. I must say more of that: perhaps now is the time.

* * *

Word having been sent to the Duchess early on that Queen Jane went about with her placket unlaced, everyone trembled to think what might happen if it proved another girl. At the same time Frances my half-sister was by then decidedly breeding. It had taken three years, despite her big hearty frame. In the end she was to bear a tiny girl, named Jane after the Queen. The Queen herself, as all know, bore a prince and died of it, or rather of a chill caught in the palace corridors after the grand christening, which she attended in a litter below wraps.

It was Lady Rochford who whispered a certain tale to me which may or not be true, but would account for little Jane Grey's persistent ill-treatment by her parents all her life; her two sisters, who came later, were not so treated, pinched, slapped and beaten often by them as Jane was always. She was very small, in that and in stubborn countenance greatly resembling the Princess Mary; these exceedingly small women have been born to the Tudors now and again since Margaret Beaufort, Henry VII's mother, whose dwarfed body held a scholar's brain. So it was with Jane Grey, and her later learning became well known. However that might have happened in any case had she been, or had she not, the King's own daughter by his niece. This was what Jane Rochford, in her spiteful way, whispered, and that the two children had been exchanged, the Queen having given birth after all to a daughter, and nobody daring to tell the King. I do not credit it altogether; Jane Rochford afterwards ran crazy, and had earlier testified against her own husband, Anne Boleyn's brother, at the trials, so could not be trusted in any case. But as such things will, the tale has stayed in my mind; supposing it happened? At that rate, Jane Grey had more right to be Queen of England than many knew; after all the Lady Mary and the Lady Elizabeth were by then both bastard, and perhaps so was she, and all three daughters by the same father. Nobody knows.

*   *   *

Meantime, with strong hopes of a living male heir, the King seemed more intent than ever on his insistence that he be acknowledged head of the Church in England, and that heads would continue to roll if he was not. One to suffer greatly then was poor Madge Douglas, whose lover or husband—nobody was ever certain which—Tom Howard died of a fever in the Tower. After the Prince's birth Madge was released, and sent alone to Syon convent, where the Bridgettine nuns had obeyed the King and signed his Oath of Supremacy. Madge never afterwards resumed close friendship with me or anyone; despite all persuasion she continued in her faith as stubbornly as the Princess Mary, who meantime had her own sufferings. She was however not put, as formerly Madge had been, directly above the place where Anne Boleyn's blood still darkened the grass below the Tower. There was great fear then in England, but while Queen Jane lived—fierce Catholics as I say had it that she was not married to the King as the marriage had not been blessed by the Pope, and that Mary was still the true heir—while that third Queen lived, there was calm on the surface. Her Grace seemed taken up with small matters apart from pleasing the King with a son; she had demanded that her ladies attire themselves with a certain large number of rich pearls studding their belts, and not all of the ladies were rich themselves. Jane Seymour's shortcomings in this way somewhat echoed her ingratitude to our young Duchess, which was not soon forgiven, for a gift of quails sent from Tattershall. Any that were sent in future, the Queen declared in a letter sent back, were to be fat, else they were not worth thanks. I myself have always loathed the killing of quails and can never bear to eat one. They blind a bird and put it in a cage, whence its cries attract the rest, which they then entrap in nets. If God's creatures are used so, what hope is there for men? Men suffered greatly at that time, and women also.

* * *

It was the same Duchess, my young stepmother Kate, who told me afterwards, when we were together again, of the christening of the King's son, which was almost the last time she attended Court for the present. As before, my father held the towel below the ewer: as before, the long-awaited baby was borne in, while trumpets brayed and Queen Jane lay exhausted where she had been carried among the pomp, with the King nearby. He was pleased with her, but during the labour, when it had been perhaps a case of saving either mother or child, had without hesitation chosen the child's life; other wives, as he truly said, could be found. Meantime the children of his former wives, now both as I declared bastard, had come in: the Lady Elizabeth, four years old, staggering under the weight of a long train borne after her by the Lady Mary. That last had greatly changed from the days when the Pearl of England, as she was called, had played her lute at Beaulieu and had declaimed Latin with her mother and my Lady Salisbury, who both loved her; now, Kate said, she was become a pallid snub-nosed thing at seventeen, a spinster praying for her dead mother's soul. No doubt she prayed for her father's also; she never ceased to love the King, who had at last forced the Princess to sign a writ declaring his own first marriage incestuous and herself bastard, having been born of no true wife. 'Master Cromwell told the King that had the Lady Mary been his daughter, he would long ago have knocked her head against the wall till it was as soft as a baked apple, so stubborn had she been,' said Kate cheerfully. Kate could be hard, and as Master Hugh Latimer had no sympathy for the Princess had none herself. The young Duchess of Suffolk was in all things the pupil of Latimer; his views moulded her far more by that time than the wisdom of my father. I myself knew that it was cruel enough to be declared bastard without being publicly degraded to carry the younger bastard's train; the priest's Anne by my mother had fortunately never had one. No doubt the royal intention had been to declare to all who watched that Mary was no longer in any way the heir of England; wronged love can turn to great hate, and he had hated the obstinacy of her mother and for the time, hated her and all who opposed his will.

As for the baby Edward, he thrived with his wet-nurse. The King visited his son often and almost worshipped him, holding him up at the window to show to passers-by. His daughters no doubt missed their stepmother; Jane Seymour had made a kind enough one, despite the pearls and the quails. It was expected that the King would marry again.

As Tom and I sat together up on the moors that day, having eaten our bread and meat and drunk our ale, my husband began to talk of the Countess of Salisbury's son, Reginald Pole, now made a cardinal.

This thought was itself strange to me, remembering him as the elegant young student who had ridden down often to visit his mother from Baliol; no doubt he would look well enough in the red hat, but it made a foreigner of a Plantagenet. Tom had seen him lately in the Low Countries, and had also formerly seen the letter Pole had openly sent to the King. Tom quoted it now, square hands clasped over his knees as he sat in the heather, gown fallen open, I glanced with affection at his revealed legs, bowed in their hose as he had described them; they were in fact a horseman's, less from Tom's own exertions in riding everywhere he must than by means of an inheritance from his grandfather, who he had already told me had been a Moravian and had come to Flanders in the train of Emperor Maximilian, Madame's whimsical father. The Moravians ride ponies all their lives, across the unending central plains, and have done so since before the memory of man; and their legs are bent to fit the saddle and the pony's sides accordingly. Likewise, Tom's baldness, which troubled him, did not trouble me; when first he had removed his cap in my presence, I had taken his head in my hands and kissed the top of it. It was not a wispy baldness, such as some men have to endure, but a great revealed symmetry of shapeliness of a skull notable as Caesar's. The hair behind was soft, straight and brown. I sat watching him now as he quoted Cardinal Pole's letter from memory, word for word.

> *You have squandered a huge treasure; you have made a laughing-stock of the nobility; you have never loved the people; you have pestered and robbed the clergy in every possible way; and lately you have destroyed the best men in your kingdom, not like a human being, but like a wild beast.*

It was every word of it true, and would duly

enrage His Majesty. I remembered saintly Fisher, with Tom More who had been the King's friend, Prior Houghton himself, and young Sebastian Newdigate who had been about Henry's court earlier, the last having as I say been chained to a wall by neck and legs, alongside his two Carthusian brothers, for two mortal weeks before being dragged out to die. Mercy Gigs, dead More's adopted daughter, had smuggled in food as she could to the three monks and cleaned up their ordure. Later on ten more of the Carthusian brothers were also chained up, and this time left to starve to death, Mercy no longer being permitted to visit them and no one else daring to. All this was for crossing the King's will.

Tom, my husband went on talking. 'The Cardinal says this ought to be inscribed on Henry's tombstone; *He has spent enormous sums to make all universities declare him incestuous.* That is the truth; no doubt it all sprang from the King's passion for Anne Boleyn, but long before that he was spendthrift, using up all his father had garnered by making war on France, hoping himself to become Emperor in his gilded armour. Now it is worse than at any time before, even abroad. Henry has sent spies, kidnappers and cut-throats to try to capture Cardinal Pole by any means. He even offered an immense army of men to our Emperor in exchange for Pole's person. What can anyone think of him who does not dare disobey him out of fear? Soon, perhaps, he himself may be made afraid. Tasting the fat priests, as he calls it, offends many.'

I recall Lady Salisbury's words to me in the Prior's garden: *Nothing will have any effect on the King's Grace but a calamity, or something that makes him afraid.*

* * *

That saying also had come by way of her son Reginald from his exile, where he had made friends of many. The other sons, Montagu and Geoffrey Pole, remained about the King at Court. I had written a note to tell my lady I was married, directing it to Warblington. I smiled to myself, knowing that she would be glad for me. It was some time since I had heard of or from her. Now, away from the constant clamour of Master Hugh Latimer about the Duchess, I could have peace to remember former times as well as present ones. I turned my head towards Tom, but he was looking ahead, long jaw intent. In the distance, a rider was making his way towards us on a short-legged pony.

'It is Christopher Askew,' Tom said. His voice held no surprise. I had never known by then, and seldom did afterwards, my husband to be taken aback by anything; his mind had made provision for all things, which faculty made him the Emperor's good servant. I stared at the oncoming knight and beyond him again to where, below, could be seen Eleanor Clifford's hastily erected wing of Skipton Castle. I began to have the feeling that we were all of us taking part in a masking with a painted curtain behind it.

Christopher Askew proved to be the uncle-in-law of that Sir Thomas Kyme who had put his wife Anne out on the road for gadding and gospelling, but Askew himself was a plain man with humble, friendly eyes. I perceived that the two men had arranged to talk together and would have withdrawn, but Askew and Tom made me stay.

* * *

'Sit down again, Mistress Blakeborn; what we have to say must be known presently by all, as it is by many here already. They say we men of the north have little fashion and less wit, so you will maybe bear with my rough speech.'

He then began to speak in a voice like a prophet, repeating the words that had been uttered lately at Louth.

'Masters, step forth, and let us follow the Cross. It is less the spoiling of the monasteries that troubles honest and devout men, than the insult to the Body of God. That was seen by all lately, when Master Cromwell's men tried to steal Louth church silver plate to take it to the

King, who hath spent and spoiled enough already. A man called out that we need a new King.'

Tom nodded gravely, and Christopher Askew said the words of the rallying cry again. *'Let us follow the Cross, my masters, for God knows whether we shall ever follow it hereafter.* We have a banner made ready with the Five Wounds of Christ, and the Host and chalice, ready to march. It is said that Christ Himself has been seen by many, though I have not seen Him myself except in the bread.' Tears rose in his eyes and Tom, seeing them, turned to me.

'You, Mag, my wife and my heart, are with us now when I say this, for you have my trust. The Emperor will aid us all he can, but must do so in secret lest the King take some greater revenge on the Princess Mary. I myself must travel shortly into Scotland, to our King's nephew there who clings to the old faith; indeed King James V dare do no other, for the Church aids him against his own nobility. Also, his mind inclines to truth, though being part Tudor, he can be cruel. I must risk my chances with him, then hope to return with news.'

'We need artillery, horses and money,' I heard Askew say, while I myself felt my heart sink at losing Tom so soon across the treacherous Border, with its robbers and uncharted morasses; but I had vowed to be no hindrance to him, so kept quiet.

'The King's army is in like state,' he told the

other now, in his usual way having informed himself of such things by whatever means. 'His Grace,' said Askew, using the old title, for countrymen are slow to change, 'will not come himself. He leaves it to the Dukes of Norfolk and Suffolk, who do not deal well together in peace, though they may in war.'

I dropped my eyelids, and gave no sign that Suffolk was my father. By now, he would be making preparations to march north. Norfolk's actions I could not foresee; he was said to be a staunch Papist, but Anne Boleyn's uncle dared not disobey the King. 'Forty thousand of our men have risen,' I heard Askew say, 'and a knight of ours, named Madeson, has gone to the King to put their view to him and to demand that preacher Cranmer, and preacher Latimer as well, be degraded as dishonouring the Host. Cranmer is married; he had a tavern-wife once called Black Joan, and now they say another in secret in Germany.' He bridled, the good man, in provincial fashion; no doubt his own life was lived purely enough. My husband remarked grimly that messenger Madeson would be fortunate to keep his head.

'Ay, he was brave,' Askew said quietly. 'Someone had to go; he knew well enough he might not come back.' His eyes fastened on me. 'Where will you go, mistress, when your husband is with King James?' he asked. 'If it would please you, my niece's unkind partner Kyme hath little children who presently lack a mother. You would be most welcome there until your own lord's return.'

'Why, Mag, it would suit you to have an eye to them; it would be like young Harry you told me of,' Tom said.

I knew he was glad to have me in safe shelter, as things were, until it was seen what would happen here in the north; it was meantime, with the marching armies everywhere, in any case impossible for me to return to my father and stepmother, Kate. Tom took me to the Kyme house, we kissed tenderly and he rode off. I did not know if I would ever see him again, and to fill my mind busied myself with Anne Askew's neglected children. Her husband was a hard man, as might have been expected; I disliked Kyme and took as little to do with him as I could. The children themselves were both subdued and pert, depending on his presence or absence. At first the eldest girl had a habit of shrilling aloud 'Praise God!' at any moment, for which her father boxed her ears, then she would cry. I persuaded her to stop calling out, not without difficulty; she told me her mother had always done it, and had said one should always say aloud what the Spirit sent.

'There is no need,' I assured her. 'God hears what men cannot. You can praise Him quietly, and not offend your father.'

'I will see. Why have you three fingers and no thumb?'

'Because I was born so.' It no longer troubled me.

Gradually things grew more peaceful and I was able to order the maids and see to the linen, which their gospelling mistress had left unmended. I could only guess then, from such of the children as did not resemble their father, that the absent mother must be beautiful, a fact I was able to witness for myself much later on, when Catharine Parr was queen. Meantime, tired by the time night fell, I would go to bed and lie and think of Tom, wondering how he fared and wishing he was beside me. Having done with my prayers for him, I remembered all he had told me about himself, apart from the Moravian grandfather. His mother had been a young waiting-woman at the Court of Charles the Bold's widow, Margaret of York, sister of the last Plantagenet kings, who had sent over Perkin Warbeck against Henry VII and with Warbeck—some say he was one of the princes supposed murdered in the Tower, others that he was the son of Duchess Margaret herself and a Flemish bishop—with him went Tom's father, and in the end, they were hanged together on the same scaffold as poor Warwick, the last being allowed the sword for his noble blood, having been kept prisoner all his life, as I have said.

'They would not call my father noble,' Tom had said. 'He was an attorney's son; they came from Blackburn, but we spell our name in the old way.' I myself liked this spelling better. Tom's mother, at any rate, had wept for his father long, and had never remarried. He himself was brought up by her in the Low Countries but never allowed to forget the English tongue, which in any case is often spoken there.

As the days passed I heard little enough of the Lincolnshire rising, which is less well remembered than the one that followed soon in Yorkshire led by a young lawyer, Robert Aske. The names Aske and Askew are so greatly alike that they may have sprung from the same, but I never enquired. Anne Askew, by now in London and trying to obtain a separation from Kyme, had gone back to the use of her name before marriage; it was as though the marriage itself had never been. Meantime I heard, from Thomas Kyme's own mouth, how books were being burnt in the market-places, and often I heard church bells ring out in alarm as they would do in a high tide in that flat country, or in sudden danger. Sir William Askew himself, Anne's father, rode back and forth, at times dining at our table; but Kyme was too cautious to join his father-in-law openly against the King.

He preferred, with relish, to pass on tales to me of atrocious happenings nearby; the sacking of the Bishop of Lincoln's palace, the murder of his chancellor and the hanging, about the same time, of the Archbishop of York's cook. 'A servant who made complaint of that was rolled in a new-killed cow's hide, and left to be devoured by dogs,' related Kyme smugly. I began to understand why his wife had been driven to preach; had he used her kindly, she might have stayed at home like other wives. Then I forgot Kyme, Anne Askew, their children and everything else. Tom returned. His mission had been unsuccessful and he was downcast; but the chief thing for me was that he was in my arms again, and safe for the time.

'King James had voyaged into France, to look for a bride; they say, however, he will not wed the daughter of Vendôme, who does not please him. I would it had been possible to know all of that before I went; no one can say when James V, King of Scots, will return.' In fact James V fell in love with the King of France's daughter, and they were married in great splendour and stayed away together in great happiness till the following year. But all this we could not know, or that the men of the Pilgrimage of Grace would wade out to the King of Scots' homeward ship at last to ask him to be King of England and aid them. He would not, but sailed on; and his young bride died in the cold of Scotland soon; but all that we heard much later. Meantime Tom whispered certain news to me in our bed, where we lay together after the children were in theirs.

'The Emperor is anxious to restore Princess Mary to her rightful place, and has assembled an army; not large, it is true, but enough, with the unrest in the north here, to weigh the balance.

'It is assembled in Zealand, and could land by water near York. They say there are more than fifty thousand Englishmen now in arms; and ten thousand priests to lead them.' His mouth was against my hair. I shivered, thinking of the earlier fate of the brave Carthusians; what would Henry Tudor do to these who took up arms? *It is not given to everyone to die for Christ.* Those had been the words of young Sebastian Newdigate as he was dragged to the scaffold; they said his face had been serene to the end.

It occurred to me to wonder what part Cardinal Pole played in all of this, and I asked my husband. I felt his hands caress my body. 'Never ask that,' he said. 'He hath but deacon's orders.' I felt him smile against me, and did not think to ask at that time what it meant; never ask, he had said, and I obeyed him, only taking delight in the renewed sharing of our bodies, the complete giving one to another that is marriage. Anne Askew on the roads, I thought, could have no notion, or she would never have left it to go preaching or any other thing; doubtless Kyme had been an unkind lover.

*   *   *

Great Eleanor Clifford had been taken by the rebels on her way back from her Bolton sisters-in-law, and would have been raped but for her rescue by the vicar of Skipton and due conveyance back to her husband's now impregnable castle. By then the rising had spread to Yorkshire and it was known that Eleanor's father and mine was in command in the south parts in Lincolnshire; the Duke was, however, less brutal than Norfolk, who used methods of great cruelty despite the Agnus Dei hung always about his neck that he had won at Flodden. The world knows what befell the Pilgrimage of Grace.

For all the Five Wounds on their banner, a device taken from the tomb of a dead knight; for all the frequent presence of a man seen on a donkey and said to be Our Lord Himself; for all the King's promises, frightened as Henry was at last by the size of the rising itself and no doubt aware of the Emperor's waiting force in Zealand against him, so that one time lawyer Aske took his place at Court as mediator, with Henry's arm flung about his shoulders as a sign of friendship, the end came as it did. The Emperor did not send his aid after all; no doubt the prospect of making war on the King, now there remained a living male heir, deterred him; there was no help either as I have said from the King of Scots, who had troubles of his own, and my father's men and Norfolk's hacked and harried and slew, and in the end Aske himself was hanged in chains above York by the King's order, taking long enough to die. His brother had been the man who rescued Eleanor. Twenty-one priests were hanged at Tyburn and in Lincoln, their bodies left to turn in the wind while crows tore at their flesh. Even the King's own herald, who had knelt to Aske with the royal arms borne on his surcoat, was hanged, drawn and quartered for that, trumpeted aloud to be the reason. The pillaging of the abbeys continued, the wanton burning of many rare and precious books, the melting down of gold and silver workmanship beyond price to make knife-handles; such things I remember learning of and seeing. But there was another thing to fill my mind about then and despite all the carnage and harm and bitter betrayal it continued uppermost in my mind and prayers, with Tom who was sometimes beside me in those days. I was with child. The discovery filled me from the beginning with wonder and dread. Kate, my stepmother, in like case again, was with my father then in the Close at Lincoln, near the destroyed Bishop's palace, and Tom conveyed me there. So circumspect was he in his comings and goings as an agent of the Emperor that it was not unsafe for him to meet my father face to face. It was the first time the two had encountered one another, and I watched the Duke's shrewd gaze dwell on us both in some fear; but my father's words held nothing but kindliness. He chaffed Tom for getting me pregnant as quickly at my age, without asking further questions. Tom looked him in the eye as he looked all men, without fear or favour, and answered wittily. I could see that the two liked one another. 'Kate will be glad of your company,' said the Duke. 'I cannot be always with her at this time.' He said no more, and I thought he himself was beginning to look an old man, though still in evident health; he had lost his teeth, but otherwise his great face was as solid as ever, his hair and beard snow-white. He told us how he had received of the King, in gift, the Valley of God, Vaudey Abbey. I knew that the last three monks left there, having remained faithful to their vows, hung now on gibbets, their bones picked bare; and dared not look towards Tom, but he made no sign. Later my father and Kate used the carved stones of the pillars to shore up their new foundations at Grimsthorpe, only one part of Kate's inheritance for which Lady Willoughby had battled and had won. Soon it was to become their home more than any other place, except for the Barbican when they were in London.

6

Tom rode off and Kate and I presently travelled in her litter to visit her mother, who was then still alive at Eresby, but far gone with the sickness which soon killed her; having done all she could for her daughter, she had no wish left to live, but only to be with her dead mistress the Queen again at Peterborough. We did not look out beyond the curtains to the dreadful sights to be seen on the road on the way but talked instead of such things as we might. I asked for young Lincoln, who was not with his parents.

'He has been chosen already as companion to Prince Edward,' said Kate. 'I miss him greatly, but there is after all this other to come.' She patted her own belly, and the gesture made me think of how the King had used to pat Queen Jane's. Kate added that the Prince continued fat and well, biting on his coral and silver ring at Havering and showing, they said, a forward intelligence already. Kate talked proudly of the great pots of silver gilt the Duke had sent as a christening gift that time trumpets had brayed, the Lady Mary had borne the Lady Elizabeth's train, and Queen Jane had caught her death-fever.

'The King is cheerful again, and visits me often masked in London,' Kate added, telling me Henry had not mourned Jane Seymour for as long as everyone thought, though he had continued quiet for a time after her death. 'He brought a portrait to show me of the Duchess of Milan which Master Holbein painted, and designed to marry her if she would take him, he said,' remarked Kate, adding in her unafraid way that Christina of Milan had however sent word since then that if she had two necks, one would be at the service of his Majesty. 'As for Madame de Longueville, who as you know hath preferred the King of Scots to our King's great wrath, she said, when King Henry told her he needed a big wife, "But my neck is small". It is easy to speak as openly when one is far away; but I find that the King laughs with me and that we deal well together.'

I looked at her pretty heart-shaped face under the new flat coif, and her gold-dusted hair, and was not surprised; the King liked comely and pretty young women, knew Kate was again proved with child and that perhaps my father would die soon in the natural way. I prepared accordingly to tremble for Kate, but she had already begun chattering of what a mercy it was that the late Popish rising had been put down by the Duke's efforts and those of old Norfolk, in alliance for once, and I made my mind turn from her alien talk to those of my own coming child. If only he had ten fingers I would be deeply happy, but the fear stayed with me all through my pregnancy that he might take after myself.

I was no longer young, and might well have a difficult birth or even die of it. That prospect brought me no fear, but a motherless boy or girl would suffer all through life, and Tom and I had made such a one together. I was almost certain, however, that my child was a boy. He sat well forward, as did Kate's. Tom wrote to me often secretly, being back again by then in Flanders. He was anxious for me to join him there for safety when it could be contrived, as our King, having acquired money again, was becoming the more capricious and cruel. He had lately ordered the burning of women and children if necessary, should they show signs of adhering to the old faith and refuse the oath concerning himself as Supreme Head.

* * *

My son was however born safely in England. I called him Anthony, after that saint who keeps very near us and finds things which are lost. Anthony had ten fingers, Tom's honest hazel eyes and stubby thick dark lashes, and when his little legs grew they were as straight as young trees, so all was well. By then, Kate also had borne her second son to my father, safely like the first. He was called Charles after his father and mine. The second Charles Brandon, though no fool, would never be as scholarly as his brother, who was soon having learning stuffed into his head at Havering, and later Ashridge, in the company of the Prince. Charles was more like the Duke, both in countenance and physical strength; even as a baby he had an iron grip, a solid countenance and blunt heavy features with penetrating eyes, not gentle like his brother's.

I was to see more of him in the end than Harry Lincoln, and taught both him and my son to ride ponies as soon they could. All this sounds smooth and pleasant; the reason it was not altogether so was that my father sent for me about then early, and gave me certain tidings I could not fail to heed.

I had been feeding Anthony, which I liked to do for myself, like the peasants employing no nurse. In my opinion great ladies miss a great deal of pleasure by trying to keep their breasts in shape, and some lose this in any case.

I loved to feel my son's small rosebud of a mouth fiercely drawing out my milk, and his perfect little hands pushing hard against my flesh, as kittens will with a mother cat. I had just finished with him for the time, cleaned myself afterwards with a cloth dipped in rosewater, and fastened up my bodice, when the Duke sent a servant for me, bidding me come to him without delay.

This summons was not like my father, who in all things was as a rule leisurely and placid, except when he had suddenly to obey the King.

He sat now in his great chair, alone; he wore a cap of black velvet, with flaps over the ears, and a heavy gold chain over his coat and tunic. Behind him on the wall hung the portrait of himself and the Queen-Duchess at the time of their marriage. Then, as now, he was massive, like a great bear full of honey. He greeted me pleasantly and bade me seat myself, which I did not, as a rule, do in his presence. I obeyed, folded my hands together on my lap and waited. I saw his close-set eyes survey me kindly.

'I am glad that you are happy, Mag,' he said, 'with your marriage and your son. He is a fine little fellow, and will I hope grow up with my own pair when this coil is dealt with; but that I must relate to you. You will wonder why you have been sent for.' He fell silent, turning a ring on his finger. I knew it was one Madame of the Netherlands had given him, that time long ago when it was rumoured that they were to be married. Despite her rumoured anger at Charles Brandon's presumption, she had not asked for the ring to be returned; he always wore it. He had no doubt loved Madame, as he had loved Mary Tudor and Anne Browne and, now especially, young Kate; and they had each one loved him in return. So, I was aware, did I. I listened as my father began, hesitantly, to speak.

'You will know that when I was young, I was poor and of no account,' he said. 'My mother had been widowed at Bosworth by King Richard, for which reason, later on, his royal niece Margaret Lady Salisbury sought me out and aided me as soon as she could, with a pension from her own purse as long as I needed it. For that reason similarly, I want to aid her now.'

'Aid her?' I thought of the Countess, as far as I knew calm and dignified at Warblington, conducting her household, her chapel, her charities, and her sons in as far as she saw them; they remained at Court except for Reginald, still abroad. I thought of the late rebellion and the Emperor's assembled army in Zealand, put two and two together and raised my good hand to my throat. My father's eyes continued to regard me keenly.

'She is in very great danger,' the Duke said quietly. 'You know that I serve the King, because I must; I would not say this even to Kate my wife, but you are older and discreet. It is like the days of our tourneying, when I had to let Henry win because if he did not, he grew pettish; and a King's envy brings death. I made play, therefore, to be less expert than I was, and great Harry rode off the victor always, well pleased, like a child. In many ways he is so; but a spoilt child, with power. After Queen Catharine lost her influence over him, no man could predict what he would do; his caprice is beyond measure, and if we want to keep our heads we must obey, at the risk of our consciences. Chancellor More preferred his conscience. So did Bishop Fisher. So, no doubt, will my Lady Salisbury.'

'What is to happen to her?' I said. 'Surely he will spare an old woman who has done him no harm. Her son the Cardinal's intrigues abroad she cannot prevent.'

'Ah, but she knows of them,' said my father. 'Do you suppose it is by accident that Reginald Pole hath never taken any but deacon's orders, which will still allow him to marry despite the cardinal's hat?

'The Princess Mary was my lady's godchild and dearest charge. They say, and I believe with truth, that Margaret Salisbury cherishes the notion that they may one day wed and unite the Plantagenet claim with the Tudor. It would please the country well enough except for the child at Havering. Edward's succession is preferred by those of the new thought; but the Princess is regarded as true heir by the rest, including the Emperor abroad, her powerful ally; and Reginald Pole is in constant touch with him and with the English malcontents in Flanders as well as the Pope.'

'But my lady—' I longed to be out of here, to ride and warn Lady Salisbury without delay of her danger; what was to happen to her that my father presently knew of. But I had to let him speak.

He put his hand down flat on the table that stood by him. 'Not all men love Master

Secretary Cromwell,' he said in a low voice. 'It is true that he toils night and day, was a faithful husband while his wife lived, and by now is an excellent host to his friends at dinner in his house at Austin Friars; nor can he help his swine's face and thick neck, which many hope may soon be severed, for a swift rise means a great fall.' My father thumped his palm on the table, which shook suddenly with his rare anger. 'But Cromwell hath brought in a law, or lack of law, that means Magna Carta might never have been signed in England. A man—or woman, Mag—can be arrested without having any offence named, and imprisoned thereafter at the King's pleasure. This is what I mean when I say the King is a spoilt child. No man who is true and just would countenance such a law in his realm. Under it, they may ride at will and take my Lady Salisbury to prison, and keep her there despite her age and high birth, and not dare speak of it any more than in the time of the King's father. I have a plan to save her, however, and here I need your help, which I know you will give.'

'Gladly,' I said. 'She hath treated me with great kindness. What am I to do?' I could see that he had plans laid, like a good commander, and I would obey like one of his men.

'Pack your gear,' said my father. 'There will be a litter waiting to convey you and your son to Warblington with as much speed as any litter may make; that is not saying a great deal, but you will need it for the child and, later, the old woman. I have a pass here, obtained from the King, for two servants of mine and a child to pass into the Low Countries. There is also clothing for the second servant, which you must induce my lady to put on. Once there, she may rejoin her son and you your husband—if you can find him.' His eyes twinkled. 'Did you suppose, Mag, that I made no enquiry about the man who married my daughter out of hand? In fact, I did not need to do so.' His face darkened. 'When I was a boy of fourteen, I stood in the crowd that watched Warbeck hang, and with him a man named Blakeborn who died bravely. That is not so usual a name but that one remembers it. Later on, at the Court of the Netherlands, I heard of one also of that name, a young man who had decided at the last minute not, after all, to become a priest. That is as well, all things being said.' He smiled. 'Now go. Here is money, and I have an escort ready for you to ride. When you are aboard ship, send the litter and men back to me for Charles and my Kate, who need them.'

I knew that I must not even say goodbye to Kate. I took the bag of leather he handed me, feeling its weight in coin, made my courtesy to the Duke, my father, and went. Within an hour Anthony and I were in Kate's litter, making our slow journey southwards. I held my son close and prayed that we might be in time.

* * *

We were not. Warblington courtyard was full at last of armed men, and before I had time to do more than emerge from my litter, carrying Anthony, I saw an old woman dragged out, showing signs of dishevelment as though they had used her roughly.

I hardly knew the Countess, her head no longer covered with the dignified headdress of the old fashion I remembered, but with a plain square cap of rabbit-skins, tied on to her head ready to ride. They mounted her on a horse and surrounded her so quickly, and rode off, that there was no time for the lamenting servants to do anything but cringe before the ready swords; none of them were themselves armed. I saw Lady Salisbury borne past on the road north, and could only hold up Anthony for her to see and bless. She knew me, smiled and made the sign of the cross over my son as she passed by. Then they were gone, and I felt a sudden hand grip my wrist. I turned in some fear; but it was Tom, my husband.

'Her son sent me on the same errand as yourself,' he said, his face grim. 'It is a pity we did not arrive sooner. They are taking her to Cowdray for further questioning. They say her steadfast courage has already been that of a man.'

We learned later, from one of the servants,

that Warblington itself had been ransacked; later it was ruined by the King's order. They had found, in one of the Countess's chests, a piece of fine embroidery on a tabard, being the Five Wounds of Christ. It was the device used lately in the north. Furthermore, there was some stitchery of pansies and marigolds, the Pole emblem entwined with that of Princess Mary. This was the excuse taken to detain the Countess, whom presently they removed to the Tower. Her brother Warwick had languished in that place for years, but in his youth, which was all he knew. Now, in her old age, Margaret Plantagenet, Clarence's daughter, last of her blood, was betrayed, and by one of her own sons; Geoffrey Pole had turned King's evidence, while Montagu, the elder, was beheaded. Had Reginald Pole been likewise in England his head would not have remained on his shoulders long; as it was, he was safe except for the King's constant spies and cut-throats, being however well guarded against these. I heard more of it in Flanders, to which we all three crossed safely, using the pass. It had not been stated whether the second servant was a man or a woman.

*   *   *

I wrote to the Duke my father about what had happened, but naming neither him nor anyone lest the letter be opened by Cromwell's men, who were kept busy as ants with unseen affairs, and the least thing reported to their master.

I may add here that Montagu's young son, a child, was taken to the Tower and never seen alive by anyone again. One hears less of that than of the two sons of Edward IV there, in King Richard's time. Thereafter followed nevertheless a season of happiness whose memory I cherish, for it was the only time in all our lives that my husband and I and our son Anthony lived together as a family, in a small curly-gabled house Tom had found for us in Antwerp. There, we could be near news from England, and there were many English in the town, besides the princely Fuggers, the Emperor's bankers who rode in and out with a clatter of stowed gold; merchants also from the old tradition of the Hansa, whose ships clustered at anchor in the port estuary. When Anthony could walk enough, I would sometimes take him to view them far off, their sails furled like pricked white dogs' ears, listening.

There was plenty of news to hear; the Emperor had ridden to quell the riots in Ghent, and Tom rode with him; my heart was in my mouth till I saw him safe at home again, for the fighting was butchery. If one man must own half the world, they could not have chosen a better than Charles V, who did his best; but not even Charlemagne could have dealt with the rising tide of Lutheran thought in Europe since before 1530, when the Emperor as a young untried man had presided at the Diet of Worms and had heard Luther himself without fully understanding, and certainly without agreement, after all the dissertations. There was no agreement anywhere except round our hearth at home, and there, at the day's end, I would listen to Tom teach his son Latin, with which tongue one may be understood anywhere in the world, and in it Anthony early became proficient, as I saw also that he did in English. I often thought of England, and my father and stepmother and their two growing boys, with whom Anthony should have grown up as a brother; and of Lady Salisbury, still held prisoner in the Tower. No news of her could be got either from England or from Italy, where her son the Cardinal remained, increasing daily in power and influence and making friends with the famous; they said he might well become Pope in due time.

Popes, Emperors and Kings; we heard of the fourth marriage of Henry VIII at last, on Cromwell's advice, to the Protestant Princess of Cleves; and that the King at sight misliked her, saying she had ill smells about her and, later, that she was not a virgin. In my opinion, Henry Tudor knew little of virginities; Queen Catharine had been married first to his brother, whatever she said later on; and Anne Boleyn had lost her treasure in this way to young Northumberland, whom she loved and who would have married her but for the King's veto; Jane Seymour her enemies said was no virgin, but I know nothing of that; and Bess Blount and Mary Boleyn and the rest were nothing to the argument. What I heard of the procession to Blackheath, following which the King proved so displeased that he would not present the Cleves princess's gift of furs to her himself, was that poor Madge Douglas rode in it, having been released at last from the Tower. She was less of a threat to the throne now Prince Edward lived. He himself was said to be, already, a phenomenon of learning, and Kate my stepmother wrote to me that her Harry kept up with him well enough. Young Charles was still at home with her and my father. I longed to see them, but while Tom was with me I was content. However the Emperor's troubles did not begin or end with Luther and Ghent. Tom came home one day with a grave face, and kissed me with particular tenderness.

'Mag, I must leave you for a time,' he said. 'A divided Christendom is bad enough; but there is still a common enemy despite the Emperor's capture of Tunis and his crushing of the corsair Barbarossa. My master says he will make war now by sea against the pirates of Algiers, and I must sail.'

I closed my eyes and clung to him. 'Whatever cause may be his is yours, as I know well,' I said. 'But it is surely too great a task for one man; there is the Council to come also that he already plans for.' This was to be the great Council of Trent, to which Reginald Pole himself would ride as president; that was not yet, and there came a time between when the King of England and the Emperor were once more made one against France, because the Turk anchored at Toulon with the French King's blessing. Everywhere there seemed to be increased turmoil, and meantime I led Tom inside and we ate bread and sausage together and after Anthony was put to bed, made love. Such times I remember as treasures to be stored in a jewel-box; and like jewels, they were rare. My husband rode off in two weeks, towards the south and the Imperial fleet.

* * *

Grief is like a stone. I had some warning of it when I awoke in the middle of one night to find Anthony out of his bed, and saw a small figure in its nightshirt standing close against the casements, which rattled ominously. I got up and went to him; beyond and high above us sailed the moon, with clouds scudding past, and a great wind had arisen, blowing towards the south. I thought of the Emperor's fleet and prayed that it would be out of danger; by now it would have set sail, surely, against this sultan they called Suleiman the Magnificent; I had had no word.

'Mother, the ships are playing ninepins,' said my son. In the moonlight we could see the crammed merchantmen set at all angles, their lamps hung askew, rocking all ways on the dark river. If confusion reigned in the sheltered port, what must it be like at sea? I took Anthony back to bed, which he shared with me in my husband's absence; it kept us both warm. He slept soon; I did not, and waited till dawn broke, then dressed myself and hurried out, still in the wind. It blew hard against my skirts and I had difficulty in making my way to the Cathedral, where even the candle-flames guttered; many women were there already, and some old men. I knelt and did as they did, praying aloud for the fleet at sea. All I know is that I had a certainty of disaster, even then, but the news itself did not come for many days.

Then it came; and the fleet was lost, scattered, ruined. Word was brought by a rider and it took longer, much longer, to know who would, and who would not, return home. I knew earlier than many. The Emperor's seneschal himself came to my door, grave-faced beneath his broad hat, and handed me a letter with His Imperial Majesty's seals. There was also a package. I read the letter. Tom was drowned. There have been romances of lovers and husbands who have been, after all, captured by the Turk, used as slaves for many years, and then ransomed in some way or else escaping, and returning home to the joy of all. Tom would never return; his body had been glimpsed floating.

I set the letter aside to read again and again, and opened the package. Inside was a small oval framed in diamonds surrounding a deep crystal, behind which was to be seen a portrait of a beautiful young woman and her son, the last having fair hair and a jutting lip; the Empress Isabella, lately dead, and Don Philip, the Emperor's heir whom his father loved greatly, and who was in Spain. My mind registered everything coldly, including this gratitude Tom's secret, constant work over the years had earned; not all widows received gifts as I had done, or a letter.

Then I sat down, and the tears would not come. I thought of Tom's body washed by the uncaring sea, sinking at last as they do, for the fish to eat, for the bones to lie forever at last on the ocean's bed, with other bones, until the resurrection. I went over all I had been taught about death and recalled how never before at any, at my mother's, even Madame's, had I felt such searing grief as I did now; yet it was still a cold thing, a denial of life. A part of my mind knew even then that life nevertheless went on; that there was Anthony, who would have to be told that his father was dead; but for a little while I, who had loved and been loved, thought of the man I had lost as if his life touched nobody's but my own, which was untrue; and the untruth itself induced me to pray. *De profundis clamavi ad te, Damine.* I said the lines over and over again, learning them by heart as the days passed, and the nights. I said other prayers, for Tom's soul, and had Mass said for it, with the thousand other Masses that were being said for lost men, lost ships, the lost hopes of Christendom.

7

The Emperor rode home. In defeat he looked as he had in victory, pale, grave, weighted down beyond his years with care and loss of his own; he had loved his wife and had had little time to spend with her while of necessity riding back and forth across his vast dominions. This loss was, therefore, not perhaps the worst Charles V had encountered; but for many of us women it was the end of our own living, the loss of the breadwinner and the lover. I clung to my son and had told him, seeing his little face grow pale. There would be no more Latin lessons, no father's knee to sit on any more by the fire, perhaps no kindness from any man again. Yet I recalled one who could be kind; also another line of the Scriptures, to which I turned increasingly in my distress. *I will arise and go to my father*. The Duke would receive me and my son kindly; and England now would surely be safe, for Thomas Cromwell was dead.

I wrote to the Duke telling him of my Tom's death and asking permission to return. A gracious letter came back as soon as might be. *Your boy shall grow up with my own two and Kate will be glad of your company,* my father wrote. He added that since the fiasco of the Cleves marriage and divorce, the King had taken a wife whom he greatly loved, a young girl, Norfolk's niece and a Catholic. *We must wish him happy, to continue as he is now,* the Duke wrote; it was safe to write such things, as my Lord Essex, as Cromwell had become, had had his thick neck severed on the block like so many he had sent there himself, and letters were no longer scrutinised as they had been. I packed my things, obtained my overseas pass for myself and Anthony, and set off when the weather had calmed. Crossing the German Sea at last I found I could not look at its grey waves; somewhere, the passing water might have caressed Tom's body, or what was left of that; all seas are, in the end, the same sea. I saw flat England loom in sight without emotion, and went ashore.

* * *

Anthony was able to continue his Latin after all, in company with that enchanting imp, Harry Brandon, Earl of Lincoln, who spoke it like a second language, and Spanish as well from his mother. He was in fact, though nobody dared say it, as forward in learning as the royal paragon Edward Tudor himself. Kate delighted in both her sons, and was glad when Lincoln could be spared from attendance on the King's, with whom, however, Lincoln was great friends; they progressed neck-and-neck under Master Cheke, the tutor, and rode together early at the tilt.

Charles was not far behind all of that, a bold-eyed little boy, still with my father's features, who excelled meantime in rumbustious fighting. Anthony, who had been brought up gently, was not on our first arrival prepared to square his fists and was soon knocked over; after that, my son learned to defend himself ably enough. This day of which I speak, the three boys were with us on the summer lawn at Tattershall, playing a game as old as the Romans, with pegs and thread. This was recreation time, before dinner. My father, old now and heavy of gait, sat in a chair with a straw hat shading his eyes and white hair, watching the two boys who had consoled him for the loss of the earlier sons. Kate, in a summer dress, was walking a little way off with her new Scots chaplain for the time, Master Alexander Seton. Parts of Seton's incessant talk floated back to me where I sat; there was overmuch of it and that too unctuous for my taste. He was a former friar full of the new zeal, ever ready with excuses as to why he had fled from Scotland, and crying down the King there unendingly.

'Your good King here, his uncle, hath sent James advice he will not heed, that he should seize the abbeys in his own realm as had been done in England, and use the lands for his benefit. James will not take advice, however, any more than he will stop raising sheep on the Border moors, an exercise which his uncle tells him doth not befit a king.'

'Maybe their wool and their meat are of use,' said Kate practically. The chaplain took no heed, nevertheless, of poor men's livings; he himself was comfortable enough with us by now.

'He fears the power of his rival nobles too greatly to take any such step in his northern realm; and for the Pope, dare not make that man an enemy.' Seton was full of the reformed doctrines, which greatly interested Kate. I did not know which way my father thought; he let her have her own way in such matters, being himself of little open religion except at moments of fear, as long ago at the time when he had been ordered to remove Queen Catharine to Somersham. All that was past; Catharine of Aragon was dead; and the present little fifth Queen kept His Grace content watching her dance, which she did all day. By night, they said, Henry could not leave her alone. My father, as though he had read my thought, spoke aloud from beneath his hat's straw brim.

'They say the King and his new Queen will travel north soon, to meet the Scots King at York. If that happens, there will needs be hosts on the way.' His voice was lazy, sleepy in the sun, and amused; he had not yet foreseen that he himself would be the royal host for a very long time, that James V of Scotland would not come to the arranged York meeting with his uncle, and that, instead, King Henry and the Court would linger at one of Kate's own houses which would need great and hurried rebuilding in order to contain them all; Grimsthorpe in Lincolnshire.

If this prospect taxed my father at his age, he gave no sign, but cheerfully set about making ready the great house in as much time as remained at his disposal. This was not much, and the building had to be done in haste, never a good thing at any time. Great stones from Vaudey Abbey, the Valley of God, now abandoned, were pilfered to support the weight of new wings; the carved pride of mediaeval craftsmen was hastily shoved in below quickly prepared stuff brought from a distance. It was by far a greater outburst of sudden building than even at Skipton, at the time of Eleanor's marriage up there.

When it was done, and the gardens raked over with quickly planted shrubs which would last the season, there was a great rounding up of red deer in the park for forthcoming royal hunts. I have never cared to watch these, watching everything always as I did again by now; the deer would have no chance to escape, being netted and caught beforehand; one heard their cries of despair and pain, and everyone who came in afterwards smelled of blood. My own son and Charles were avid to go, but considered too young and to be kept out of danger, which suited me. Later I watched the dancing, particularly that of the little Queen, Catharine Howard. She seemed a happy little creature, as much so as Kate herself had been when married to a man much older than herself. Her Grace moved joyously now to the rebecks and viols, her wide square bodice's neck displaying breasts mature for her age; she wore the neat round hood which was becoming fashionable. The King watched her constantly from where he sat, and often fondled her in public. For a time, everyone seemed content; there was no haste to meet the King of Scots, nor move to leave Grimsthorpe for York. The Court lingered, and old Norfolk's cold eyes dwelt constantly on this second niece made royal. It was no pleasure to him, any more than to my father, that they should be guest and host to one another, but expediency was everything. One woman close about the young Queen was Jane Rochford, George Boleyn's widow, whose tongue was always ready. In the days of Anne of Cleves, when that placid innocent creature told her ladies how the King would say to her nightly 'Goodnight, sweetheart,' and in the morning, 'Farewell, darling,' and no more, Jane had said 'Madam, there will have to be something more than that if we are to see a Duke of York.' Now German Anne was gone, known only as the King's beloved sister, in her own establishment at Richmond and Ham, but in plain fact a hostage, prevented from returning home to Germany. So many were absent from the dancing here, so many remembered faces seen no longer, their names no more spoken. I knew Lady Salisbury was still in the Tower; when I could, I thought, I would ask the young Queen if I might visit her. Meantime, I sat and listened to the gossip after my charges were in bed.

Frances Brandon, pregnant again, this time certainly by her husband, stayed nearby, too heavy by now to dance but never laggard of tongue. She spoke grudgingly of Kate's two boys; they had disappointed her of her inheritance.

'They are fine boys enough; a pity their title is not sound.' Her voice was grating, and Kate herself, who moved nearby, heard it and left the dance. She had begun to abandon gold-dust in her hair, and wore plain dark clothing, in contrast to most of the Court. It suited her; her face had acquired a grave scholarly beauty, but her wit was as ready as Jane Rochford's and she could answer back swiftly.

'Their title is sound enough; why would it not be? On my side they have the blood of the Comtes de Foix, who gave a queen to Aragon.' She smiled with closed lips, retaining her partner's hand. I stared at Frances, whose heavy jaw was growing thick. It occurred to me that, in appearance and appetites, she must resemble her aunt the Queen of Scots, Madge's mother whom I had never myself seen and who was lately dead. Frances answered Kate now with malice. 'Why, my father married many women, one of them being yourself, while Mag's mother, yet another of them, was still alive. The Pope denied the marriage at my own royal mother's request, but no one now in England heeds the Pope.'

'Perhaps we all have our uncertainties,' riposted Kate, sharp as a needle. 'After all, your own Dorset could be considered as having married Arundel's daughter instead of yourself, a betrothal being as binding as a marriage. It was perhaps the doubt about your own birth that procured you so doubtful a bridegroom. We are all of us children of Adam and Eve.' She smiled, and moved on, rejoining the figures of the dance; her own little figure in its dark gown was elegant. Frances had reddened, and for once fell silent, after saying 'That is a little bitch my father has married at last,' to which I made no reply. Despite her sharp tongue, it was impossible not to be fond of Kate; and both her boys I loved as my own.

Madge Douglas also was present that day, a stiff unhappy personage twenty-five years old by now, whom no man would be permitted to marry as far as one could foresee. She had fallen in love again with Charles Howard, kin to her dead Lord Thomas, but their marriage had not been permitted by the King and this time they led separate lives, for fear of the Tower.

* * *

The old Duchess of Norfolk was at loggerheads with her Duke and, therefore, a friend meantime of my father and favourably disposed towards myself; she obtained me an interview with the little Queen, her granddaughter, in order that I might ask the latter to intercede with the King to grant me permission at last to visit Lady Salisbury.

All this is pompous; but I have no memory other than of a smiling, loving little creature, happy to grant my request. At Grimsthorpe, I had passed up and down by night often enough at the newel stair, and had seen no man waiting there as they claimed afterwards had happened, nor heard any sounds of lovers; had I been asked to give evidence at the Queen's trial, which I was not, I could have said no other. In any case nothing could have saved

Catharine Howard; she was doomed, having been neglected young by those who should have had an eye to her, and seduced by her music-master at the age of fourteen. The King would merely have put her away for that, not had her head, when he first heard; it was Cranmer who told him, and that faction claimed also that Catharine Howard had been unfaithful since her marriage, which meant death; nothing less would satisfy them but the blood of a Catholic Queen, and a Norfolk.

Poor child; after the sound of her screams when she had tried that last time to reach the King and failed, and had been dragged away, the musicians came as usual to play for her in her chamber and were told it was no more a time to dance. Jane Rochford, who ran crazy this time as well she might, being accused of bringing the young man Culpeper by night to meet the Queen, having endured the appalling Boleyn trials and now this, kept the phrase in her mad mind and they remember kept saying aloud 'No more a time to dance, no more, no more, no more a time, a time to dance.' On the block, after Catharine herself had been beheaded, Jane Rochford regained her calm, and died a Catholic, as had her young mistress.

All that was to come; but I chiefly remember Catharine Howard smiling and moving her small full-breasted body a little, always, as if she danced still, for her skirts swayed; and saying she would gladly speak to

His Grace, and that the old lady herself should surely have a furred gown and warm petticoats to wear in the chill of her cell. These were sent indeed; Her Grace did not forget. They arrived on the same day I saw my lady, the Countess of Salisbury, once more.

* * *

I had heard nothing of her since the day I had held Anthony up for her blessing as she rode past a prisoner out of Warblington. I knew that, whatever her condition, she would behave always with calm courage; as they had said at the time of her questioning, a strong and constant man rather than a woman; but women have courage of their own. All her long life had been passed under the shadow of the Tudor threat to the last living Plantagenets; her brother Warwick, Buckingham and Courtenay of Exeter, the last two brought up in the King's own chamber, were gone, and Lady Salisbury's own eldest son Montagu. Geoffrey Pole remained hangdog at Court, a traitor never daring to raise his eyes, and no man would trust him again. Reginald the Cardinal was still abroad, having made friends with the famous there, Vittoria Colonna, Michelangelo, the Emperor, the Pope himself.

There would have been nothing he could do for his mother in any case, had he returned to England; he would merely have lost his own life. Cromwell was dead, but the grip of the dead hand stayed; arrest was still possible without stated reason of any kind.

*　　*　　*

I left behind the sight of the busy Thames, the wherries and coal-boats and great gliding barges of the nobility with their painted prows; and was led through a gate to the inner Tower, then down steps to the place where they evidently kept my lady; it was so dark there that it might not have been a summer's day outside; the stone struck chill in the passages. A lock grated and I perceived in the half-dark a hunched and aged woman seated in a chair in a cell. I drew a breath, and ran to Lady Salisbury. She tried to rise, and for pain could not. 'My bones ache,' she said, smiling. 'It is damp in here. I am glad to see you, Mag.' The eyes looked up at me from where she sat, unchanged in their shining honesty and lack of fear. I knelt on the ground by her; there was no second chair.

We talked. I told her of Tom's drowning, my coming home, and Anthony, saying that he was soon to go to be companion to Lincoln and the Prince. I noticed that Lady Salisbury was wearing over her shoulders the nightgown lined with fur, one of the warm petticoats on her body that the Queen's Grace had promised, and a gown of worsted. They had come only last week, she told me, to warm her, from the Queen. 'She hath a good heart, that child. I knew it when I saw her once, long ago after her mother, Jocasta Howard, had died and she herself was the youngest in a large family of brothers and sisters. Later she went to her grandmother. She must be the smallest of all the King's wives, and he so large a man.' Her smile grew, the long face breaking into wrinkles.

I caressed her hands, which had once been shapely and beautiful; now, the joints of the fingers were swollen with rheumatism and to move them was no doubt difficult. I wondered that even the King would not have mercy on so old a woman; when I left here, I would, I thought, approach Her Grace again; perhaps the discomfort of the prison was not fully known.

Meantime, I answered Lady Salisbury's eager questions; first of all, how was the Princess Mary? I answered that I knew as much as anyone, which was little enough. 'She keeps herself quietly, troubling no one.'

'Her time will come,' said the Countess calmly. 'She is the true heir.' Her lips, which were purple with the cold, folded in decision, and I made no comment; few in England would openly deny the right of Prince Edward. We talked instead of Grimsthorpe, of the Suffolk family there, the royal visit to the north and the King's anger when his nephew of Scotland had failed after all to keep the rendezvous at York. 'James Stewart is capricious, they say, but he may have been afraid,' said the Countess. 'Kings of Scotland have been taken hostage by us before now.' She sighed a little, thinking no doubt of her own time in prison, the surveillance of her whole life.

There came the rattle of keys. 'They have given me but a short time with you, Mag,' the Countess said resignedly. 'There was much I had to say; word to send to my son Reynald, all manner of things to yourself, but they must keep.' She raised her head, expecting the gaoler, but it was the Lieutenant of the Tower, his face grave; halberdiers were behind him as if they had been needed for a strong man who would fight.

'My lady of Salisbury,' he said, 'prepare yourself to die within the hour. It is the King's command.'

* * *

I had risen. The Countess also tried to rise, and achieved it, standing with her tall height almost as it had used to be, having wrenched her stiff joints and balanced against my arm. I heard her say 'What is the charge?' and was told that there was none known, that it was the King's will; and at that, Margaret Pole crossed herself.

'May I have a priest?' she said, but was told there was no time. She turned to me then, ignoring the officers.

'Leave me, Mag,' she said. 'I would wish to be alone for such leisure as is left me, with my God, who has been constantly with me in this prison and whom I must soon now face.'

I left her standing there, having kissed her ruined hands. Later, they carried her out in her chair, as she could not walk as far. I was waiting, with a few others who had somehow heard the news, outside on the May grass to watch Margaret Plantagenet die. It was the most terrible of deaths, lacking even dignity. The headsman was young and inexperienced, an apprentice. He faced this old woman with the clear unafraid eyes and told her to kneel. A royal personage at the point of death was not to be addressed so. The Countess struggled up from her chair, and stood tall and accusing; it was the young man who was afraid. 'I kneel to my God and to my King,' she told him. 'Why should I kneel to you?'

There followed a grotesque parody, a dance of death; the old limbs, racked with age, of a sudden moving, running, evading the flailing axe which the scared boy began to wield wherever he could, hacking at her shoulders, her neck, her grey head they had meantime bared. It was like the butchery of a runaway animal; the crowd gasped in horror, some in enjoyment, for there are such, those who go to watch the baiting of blinded bears in a pit, of badgers with their hind feet cut off, attacked by dogs. The terrible proud eyes, blind with blood, led Margaret Pole in a doomed circle, swaying, lurching, falling at last like a felled doe, when he finished her off, the finest great lady in the land, a blood-boultered heap by now on the green grass, last of the old race which had ruled for four centuries. The crowd gave its final gasps of horror and pity, then drifted away. I knelt down by the Countess's body; her blood stained my skirts; and said a prayer for her soul. The apprentice had seized the head by its hair and had taken it away.

*　　　*　　　*

They said Cardinal Pole, when he heard the news at Viterbo, was silent for instants. Then he raised his head, in which the levelled eyes were like his mother's. 'I was proud,' he said, 'to be the son of one of the best and most honoured ladies in England. Now I am the son of a blessed martyr. God's will be done.' Then he went into his oratory and prayed for a long time, alone.

*　　　*　　　*

I almost disliked Kate my father's wife when I brought her news of the death. She was smug, being under the spell of her preacher still. 'Do you know what Master Latimer wrote when my Lady Salisbury was arrested?' she said. 'He told me of it. "Pole must now eat his own heart and be as heartless as he is graceless". Do you think indeed she plotted to marry him to the Lady Mary?' I excused myself, and went out of the room. It had taken all my control not to answer as sharply as she.

The Queen's matter followed shortly, but that was a clean death, though the victim this time was young. They say the King became an old man thereafter; he was in any case unwieldy, for he could take less exercise than before as his leg pained him, from an ulcer got in Jane Seymour's time by falling from his horse, or others said from pox. Half England prayed for him to die, but he lived on.

Whichever wife he took next would have to be his nurse. My father still lived, so it could not be Kate, otherwise it might have been. The King had used to enjoy visiting her masked, and they would laugh together. His son thrived, and was said to be a fine child; I did not go with Anthony when he was sent to Havering, and knew I would miss his company, but I was long since accustomed to being alone.

8

'I bring the evangel,' Master Alexander Seton the former Scots friar had announced, adding that the law of God had never been truly taught and that the Pope was corrupt, which may have been true. Within a few years, Seton himself was dead of phthisis, not having been saved from it by his evangel. In fact he reverted to the Catholic Church on his deathbed. They said, naturally, that he was forced to this, but men were not so forced in those times. The King considered himself as good a Catholic as any, although he had replaced the Pope by his own image as far as he might.

The Duchess was, therefore, dependent for instruction on Master Latimer, who had a great many other demands on his time, until John Parkhurst came. He was later chaplain to Queen Catharine Parr. Hangmen and papists, he declared, dealt equally in blood. About Kate herself, whose mind was being increasingly formed and made adamant by these reforming preachers, he wrote then or later *Aeternum salve, princeps clarissima mentis, dotibus, eximiis ad numeranda viris vix dici poterit.* No doubt she deserved it; she gave patronage to such men, and was almost at once close friends with the new Queen, whose views were similar. Kate in her dark gown, and I myself in my black, were bidden to Madge Douglas's wedding at last, to the renegade Scot, the Earl of Lennox; to have the English King's niece as a bride was a reward to him for waging future war on the Borders against James V's courageous widow, who refused to send her infant daughter, their Queen Mary, to England to wed our Prince. All that seemed far away, but I was pleased to see that Madge was much taken with her bridegroom, who was handsome and golden-haired although his eyes were too close-set for my taste.

The Princess Mary was present; she and the bride were friends. I hoped that Madge would be happy; we saw her bedded, with her long fair tresses combed loose about her shoulders. She was thirty and it was time that she was married.

Her uncle, George Douglas, continued to read the Bible aloud to everyone as though it were an inn-bill. He was a man of rough manners, her father's brother, and nevertheless aped the English way of speech although it was not natural to him. He constantly asserted what they all did, that the Bible had for the first time been made available to the common man lately; but not all common men could read. For this reason, the Church had always read out selected lessons as part of the Mass. I held my peace about all this reform, as the Queen and Kate favoured it and my son also was by then in the hands of Prince Edward's advisers, among them Hugh Latimer himself. I did not want to endanger Anthony's future, and kept silent when perhaps I should have spoken. I was by now good Mistress Blakeborn, in her widow's weeds, coming and going about the Suffolk household, doing what I could to aid my father, who had meantime grown almost as unwieldy as the King.

* * *

The King's ulcer was dressed twice daily by his sixth Queen. She was a beautiful little woman with, at that time, a determined mouth and glance; later her mouth grew loose and exhausted and she took to white-leading her face. She had been married before to one old husband after another, the King himself being the third; neither by word nor look did Catharine Parr ever reveal, while Henry lived, that she was long in love with a younger man but dared not show it, remembering Catharine Howard's fate.

This man, as all later became aware, was Tom Seymour, a swaggering fellow and brother to the late Queen Jane; he was accordingly much about the young Prince, and my Anthony knew him well and often joked with him. As far as the King's children by three marriages went, Queen Catharine Parr was kind to them; the Princess Mary was brought altogether out of her retirement and returned to Court, where Kate played cards with her. The red-haired Elizabeth, Anne Boleyn's daughter, by now shared a tutor, Master Cheke, at Ashridge with her young half-brother, Lincoln and Anthony and, by now at times, Charles. She outstripped all of them, being four years older than any and having in any case a mind like a sharp-cut diamond, adept at Greek. Anthony told me, with awe, that the Prince once rescued Elizabeth when her horse ran into the river at Richmond; they continued fond of one another. There was another little girl named Jane Dormer who shared the studies at that time, and Robin Dudley, who was admittedly better on a horse. Altogether they were a happy enough parcel of young people. Frances's tiny daughter, Jane Grey, was seldom allowed to join them, which was perhaps as well; her learning outstripped even Princess Elizabeth's and Jane herself was priggish, with a mind, even then, fixed on reform.

One more servant of the Duchess I will mention. He was a middle-aged man named Richard Cranwell who had for long served Kate's mother at Eresby, and when she died in 1539 came to us. He was unexceptionable in appearance, of the kind one passes by in the street without notice. He was in the house for some time before he approached me quietly and confided to me that he was a priest who had never signed the Oath of Supremacy. After that, I, and some of the servants, went secretly to his Masses which were held in a closet in the house. We were silent concerning it, not desiring Father Cranwell to share the fate of the Carthusians and the rest. As to the remaining brothers, he told me privately that they had been badgered, starved and tempted in all ways by Cromwell and his officers until in the end, after much resistance in their own minds and conscience, subtle persuasions from bribed monks sent from Syon who had conformed, and the endless disturbing of their peace, they had at last signed the oath to their own deep shame, and as soon as they could fled the country, those few who were left. Thereafter, in Flanders, they were abandoned to such quiet as they could find in their hearts; it is not given to all, as young Newdigate put it, to die for Christ.

At any rate, the day was to come when not only I myself, but the Duchess of Suffolk, were to thank God for Richard Cranwell, who helped remove her from great danger; but that time was not yet. Meanwhile, I had the comfort of kneeling before the true Host that had sustained England for fifteen hundred years and now must be kept in hiding. I was comforted, as I had been that day long ago by the side of Lady Salisbury at the Charterhouse Mass, when the whisper of God Himself had sounded through the church. Also, I knew within myself that my Countess's own calm spirit, after the torments of her body, was at peace.

*   *   *

It was my fault and nobody else's that Anne Askew the preacher I had heard of in the north was taken to the Queen, for I myself brought her at last to my Duchess, who had heard of her also and was curious to meet her, and thereafter sent her money, of which commodity Anne was short, living by now as she did in London and still suing for her divorce from Thomas Kyme. I had sent for one of the young Kyme children from Lincolnshire as soon as it might be done, for the girl was slightly lacking in her wits and I knew might come to harm without her mother. Unfortunately she had her father's face and her mother's disposition, and unless beaten would learn nothing; but at least I taught her to sew. I knew Anne Askew's direction, because most folk did, and that she was likewise often to be seen and heard about St. Paul's. I told her her daughter was with me at the Barbican, and she came to see her, but the child hardly remembered her mother by now and only stared dully at this strange woman who was said with some truth to resemble an angel; certainly Anne Askew was beautiful of feature, but had a mad gleam in her eye, as might have been expected, and a too-constant smile as though convinced of her own unvarying righteousness. I took her in to meet Kate, and Anne began at once to preach the evangel. I might have foreseen as much, and that the two women would take to one another accordingly. My father was absent, being with the King who often sent for him and who, despite his royal ulcer and old age, planned a war again with France.

I think that had the Duke been present, the talk might have taken a less headlong turn, but as it was, Anne and Kate started discussing Coverdale's great Bible and how the King of France had burned the first copies after allowing them, but the presses were smuggled across to England, 'and now it is here for all to read,' said Anne Askew joyfully. 'If I may, I will bring Your Grace a copy.' There was no more mention of her poor afflicted child, who had stayed on with us meantime. The Coverdale copy was brought, and became one of Kate's cherished possessions. Later on, heavy as it was, it travelled with us all into Poland. Meantime, Kate spoke of Anne Askew to the Queen; and she, whose second husband, Lord Latimer, had been one of the leaders of the Pilgrimage of Grace, hearkened to the evangel as given forth by Anne and Anne thereafter frequented the Court on more than one occasion.

I was bidden there that winter also to play at

mumchance with the Princess Mary, Lady Madge Lennox who was thickening with her first child, and Kate herself. The King and my father talked and laughed together at a second table where sat Lady Tyrwhitt, the Queen's stepdaughter, and the Queen. I marvelled again at the likeness between the two big men, both white of beard by now, both amiable for the time, but my father after all was seldom otherwise. Great chains such as Norfolk wore lay about their tremendous shoulders, plump hands grasping the cards on which, after the new pattern over late years, were portraits of the King himself and Queen Catharine of Aragon in her long hood, replacing the old bells and leaves and acorns folk had used formerly. No doubt His Majesty had not thought to order the design to be changed with each successive queen.

The Countess of Lennox, in a carnation satin gown made no doubt by Master Peter her dresser whom I know of, began to deal. I stared beneath my lids at her and at the patient Princess, as the Emperor himself called Mary Tudor; marvelling at how colourless and submissive the latter had become although she always liked to wear bright clothes. The news that Lady Salisbury had been hacked to death must have reached her in all its unspeakable detail; she had behind her the years of resistance to her father for her mother's sake, then capitulation at last, which was the more bitter for all that had gone in vain before. Her life had been made intolerable until she had signed that denial, but I knew she would never forgive herself for betraying her dead mother. Her mouth by now had formed itself into that of a woman stubborn in her conscience. She and Madge remained close friends, in religion as in all things. I saw the three marriage-brooches the Princess had given Madge on her marriage to the handsome Earl, renegade Archer of the Scots Guard of France, whose own father had been done to death in Lennox's boyhood under Douglas power; but Madge herself seemed happy. The brooches were linked by gold chains, as was the fashion, swinging in loops above her proudly pregnant belly. The carnation colour did not greatly suit her fairness or her condition, but Lennox was absent on the King's mission to destroy the Scots. I hoped Kate, the only firm Protestant in our four, would keep quiet about the Coverdale Bible, but she did not; and tactlessly prattled on about that and about Anne Askew, and that the Queen liked her greatly and disputed with her often concerning the new evangel, and was trying to interest the King perhaps at this very moment. At that, Princess Mary raised her eyes from the cards and gave Kate a straight look, and that look was full of unforgiving hatred; it discounted the fact that Kate's own mother had been the one to ride at the last to be with the dying Queen Catharine herself, and was by now, they said, buried at her feet.

I forget how the game ended; I think Madge smoothly interposed with talk of her own lord, who was in the north meantime, fighting his countrymen, but who she hoped would rejoin her soon in time for the birth of her child, who, if he proved a son, would be called Lord Darnley.

* * *

'The great ship that lately went down, the *Mary Rose*, was named for my wife the French queen; that is partly why His Grace feels its loss so keenly, though it was a fair ship enough. She was always his favourite sister, despite our marriage and his anger at it, for she could have gone to King Francis or the Emperor, being the fairest prize in Europe; but she preferred myself. What could I have done else but marry her after she so wept? I never saw a woman so weep.'

The Duke my father, resembling a great solid rock, his hair and beard snow-white, his eyes sunken in flesh, sat in his chair gazing out of the window at the green Guildford landscape, across which the arrays of armed men sent from Woking moved steadily now for the King's French war. I knew my father was not thinking of that, or that he himself had been put in command even at his age and state of health, but, as old men do, was remembering earlier things; his royal wife, whose body lay now reburied in St. Mary's graveyard after the despoiling of the great Abbey nearby. Then he turned his notable head and smiled a little. 'Our sons died,' he said, 'but Kate hath given me others. I think of them often, racing one another up and down the passages at Grimsthorpe with its smell of new plaster making everyone cough. They will carry on my name.'

I wondered if he himself expected to die at Boulogne, where the King's order had lately bidden him go.

His Grace—my father still did not remember to call him Majesty at all times, and was one of the few of whom the lapse would be forgiven—perhaps having taken a new lease of life with his marriage, had donned sailor's wide breeches of cloth-of-gold to hide his ulcer, and was straddling the decks as he had used to do, ready to sail once more against France as in his youth. As for the Duke, he seemed unperturbed at the prospect of having to take himself likewise again across the Channel; the hands which had caressed so many women lay calmly on the hilt of his sword. I reflected, not for the first time, how Charles Brandon was exactly as old as the dynasty; born in Bosworth year, watching, as he grew, the Tudors consolidate power, garner money, spend it again on war, and, by the end, grasp more power than kings had ever before known, changing Christendom itself.

Now there was young Edward to succeed, and Kate told me the new Queen wrote the King loving letters; Henry had made her regent in his absence, and she managed the task ably.

'No Frenchman sank the *Mary Rose*,' I replied to my father; the Queen-Duchess was so seldom spoken of now that I did not want to abandon mention of her even to talk of the Duke's boys whom I loved. 'It was a strange act of God; she sank for no reason to the sea's bottom, with much stuff of value aboard.'

'The French have invaded the Isle of Wight,' grumbled my father. I replied, to cheer him, that the women of that island had taken arquebuses and fired them, and stones and thrown them, and driven the French back. He smiled again, his mouth drawn in with its recent lack of teeth.

'It is strange to think of women making war,' he said. 'They should be gentle creatures. The English in Calais would have stoned us, I remember, Mary and myself, when we passed through after our secret hasty marriage; we had to hasten, lest she be hurt. She was carrying my child by then, Frances. We called her for the new French king, to placate him, and Eleanor for his queen, later. Now we are again at war.'

He began to speak of Kate then, as if

bringing himself back to the present. 'Swear that you will have a care to her when I am gone,' he said. 'She is forward, growing set in her opinions, and will not hide them; she gets that obstinacy from her Spanish mother. I fear lest in time to come, when in nature I am no longer with her, she may meet with harm; one may never know which way the wind will blow now in England.' He regarded me suddenly with a look of great love. 'Stay with her, Mag, I beg,' he said. 'You have wisdom, maybe not all of it taught by Madame. I know more of your doings than you think; say naught of that and nor will I.'

I flushed with pleasure; it was not often my father took such heed of me as he had lately, since the death of my half-sister Mounteagle of whom he had remained fond, though he knew her to be rapacious. As for Powis, even he had abandoned her; she was a wanton, and not well regarded by anyone. I promised the Duke that I would stay with Kate; there seemed no reason not to, and they had welcomed me together when I returned, a widow, from Flanders with my son.

* * *

That talk of ours was the Duke's *Nunc Dimittis*; there was to be no expedition against Boulogne. Next day he took a seizure, and shortly died, so quickly that few even on the

Council knew that he was ill. Kate was in time to be with him, also Frances, and Eleanor. It had not been possible to send for his sons. When they brought the news to the King he was reported to be in great grief. They say Charles Brandon was the only man in all his life Henry VIII really loved; they were similar in many things, except that my father was not cruel by his own will. However His Majesty paid a worthy tribute to the Duke in Council. 'He never attempted to injure an adversary, or whispered a word to the disadvantage of anyone, in all the course of our friendship,' he told them; and looking round the faces assembled, greedy, avid, pretentious, jostling always for advantage, playing one off against another, added with shrewdness, 'Is there any of you, my lords, who can say as much?' My father had asked to be buried quietly at Tattershall, which he had loved; but it was not to be. The King gave him a funeral of great pomp and interred his body in St. George's Chapel, Windsor, where he himself would lie. *Voide of Despyte* was my father's motto. Unlike the Queen-Duchess with hers, he had lived up to it. I missed his presence greatly; so did Kate, who cried for a time.

The boys had been gently told of the death and had wept, for they loved their father. Young Harry was now Duke of Suffolk. The two were brought solemnly to the funeral, then both returned to the Prince. That young man, aged eight, was to be seen in public for almost the first time, his father having formerly kept him close, on the occasion of the visit of the Admiral of France, the very man who had lately attacked the Isle of Wight, in state to Hampton Court. It was a sign that the King was not well; his ulcerated leg was said to be laid daily in the patient Queen's lap and he seldom walked nowadays without being conveyed in a chair from room to room; they said that when he was enraged his face turned black.

Accordingly, it was as if to watch the rising sun that we waited to see young Edward, in crimson-and-white satin, his yeomen in cloth of gold, with a further eight hundred yeomen of the guard behind, ride out on a charger to Hounslow. Beside him was Archbishop Cranmer, his usually tense countenance pleased; Queen Jane's brother, Hertford, with his solemn long beard, and the Earl of Huntingdon. The young Prince exchanged kisses with the reconciled M.d'Annebaut and then, marvellously, made a speech himself in French which everyone could hear. 'He has not been learning it for long,' breathed Anthony in my ear. 'He is most apt to learn.' He loved Edward, as most people near him did, including Edward's own terrible royal father. Later, there was a ceremonial ride back, with the Admiral's right hand under Edward's left, still both mounted and their mounts under control; then more formal progress, through the passages of the great palace that had once belonged to Cardinal Wolsey, exchanging of compliments and gold and silver plate, and all that week banqueting, masks, and jousting, with the old royal invalid showing himself sometimes after all. It was September, fine weather, and everyone I believe felt that the shadow of the dying reign would soon be lifted, and a new age begin. I was glad that my son had ridden with the new Duke of Suffolk to Court, though I missed the boys' company still. Shortly thereafter, there was of course the fearful arrest of Anne Askew, which almost resulted in the death of the Queen herself.

9

There was a party which desired the downfall of Catharine Parr as strongly as the opposing party, before that, had seen to the downfall of Catharine Howard; and before that again of Cromwell, so that it was like a devil's game of tennis, one side Catholic, the other Protestant, each having its victims and plotters and martyrs. I myself know only that Christ gave St. Peter and his successor the power to loose and bind, and there seemed to me nothing more clear-cut than that; but if one were to say so, it would be to share the fate of Fisher,

More, the Carthusians, the friar roasted alive in his iron cage, and the numberless corpses hanging still on gibbets from the Pilgrimage of Grace. I am no martyr, as I know well, and I held my peace, partly for the sake of my son. Kate did not hold hers; as my father had predicted, she was becoming daily more outspoken and seemed to fear nobody. Her particular dislike, as I have no doubt said already, was Bishop Gardiner of Winchester, after whom she had named her dog because, as she said, she could kick him at that rate once a day at the least. This made me sorry for the dog, but God's creatures have little mercy shown them.

Kate and the Queen, and the Queen's sister Lady Pembroke, and her stepdaughter Lady Tyrwhitt who had played that time at cards, were all in a knot to discuss theology aloud at any hour, which the Queen also did in the King's closet, and at first the King was diverted by it. As the time passed, however, I believe even he began to realise the harm he had done in his realm, and he was heard to pronounce that the Bible, that precious jewel of the word of God, was disputed, rhymed, sung and jangled in every ale-house and tavern, contrary to the true meaning and doctrine of the same. This pronouncement should have warned the Queen had she been wary, but she was not given to suspicion then and had not taken thought how every word she dropped, and her admiration of and, in her constant speaking out, imitation of Anne Askew herself would be used against her by those who held it to be in their interest to destroy her.

Norfolk, despite his harshness in the Yorkshire rising, was a Catholic and adverse to doctrinal discussion, and no doubt to anything at all said by women; he was in any case of a sour disposition in all ways. On his side was Chancellor Wriothesley and Bishop Gardiner himself. Against them was Cranmer, who had broken the news to Catharine Howard that she must die and had earlier told the King she was unfaithful. It was said already that the sound of her screaming could still be heard at certain times in the palace passages. I did not myself hear it. Anne Askew had given the Queen books on theology as she had given them to Kate, and present at the time had been her sister and stepdaughter as I say, also little Lady Jane Grey, who had been taken away meantime from her unkind parents and kept about Court. She was nine years old, and used to carry candles before the Queen, her tiny figure even smaller than Catharine's own. The King preferred small women, which was partly why Anne of Cleves had displeased him. Nevertheless, he had been brooding for some days, and those who knew him well enough were aware that this was when he was most dangerous. The Queen took no heed if she noticed it, and continued as usual, diverting

His Majesty, as she thought, with further dissertation about matters of doctrine, not knowing yet that officers had come and taken Anne Askew away to question her, and that most horribly by torture. They say the Chancellor himself took off his coat to rack her; she said later that he almost plucked her joints asunder. I had never been inveigled by Anne, remembering always her neglected children in the north; but there is no doubt that she was brave. Nor would she, as they wanted her to do, name the Queen in anything, or the Queen's friends. It is a marvel to me that Kate escaped suspicion. At that time the King had a favourable eye to her and paid her much attention, as if he would make her his next wife. No doubt that saved her; she was proven fertile, which Catharine Parr was not, by any of her three husbands. Barrenness might have been the excuse to get rid of her earlier had she not been so excellent a nurse to the King's ulcerated leg.

Now, there was the added excuse of browbeating the King over religious matters as, no doubt, in her reforming zeal, the poor lady had done without deliberating the matter. When in argument, she inclined in any case to be downright when subtlety would have served her better. She learnt this presently, but at a cost. They might have had her off to the Tower, for it was arranged for the next day except that, in the gallery at Whitehall, a paper already signed by the King fell out of Wriothesley's coat. It was quickly picked up and shown to the Queen, who broke down in hysterics. She already knew of the fate of Anne Askew whom they had meantime burned at Smithfield and who had died with great courage, carried there crippled in a chair, the smile still on her face despite a second racking. They had set off bolts of gunpowder in order that she might die quickly, and this alarmed Gardiner and Wriothesley, who sat nearby. I was reminded of the jeering of Hugh Latimer over the roasting of John Forrest in his cage; fooling over the friar, Latimer had called it. Gloating over death by torment is unspeakable, whichever side one is on, and there is no need for arranged death to be anything but clean.

The Queen's screams disturbed the King, who had not heard those of Catharine Howard, or Anne Boleyn in her time in the Tower. Inconvenienced, he had himself carried into Catharine's room in a chair. At sight of him the Queen exerted her considerable wits and, in the end, saved herself by deferring to Henry as lord and master and admitting that she was but a woman, with all the imperfections and weaknesses of her sex. 'Of you, next to God, will I ever learn,' were the words which began to placate the monster, and the statement that it was preposterous for a woman to instruct her lord put matters right again between them. The King ended by calling Wriothesley a very knave, and peace reigned at Court once more, as far as it might do so, but it was after that that Catharine Parr began to use white lead on her face, and to have haunted eyes and a mouth that trembled always.

Wriothesley being suspect, Norfolk, my father's unfriend, was likewise; he and his son Surrey were shortly arrested and sent to the Tower. The latter was a poet, albeit a noisy young man who broke windows. The Seymours, Queen Jane's brothers, resented him in turn, and persuaded the King that Surrey had plotted to give him a mistress, none other than the young Howard widow of Henry's own bastard son Richmond. The implication of incest was enough, having been begun and ended with by the King in his marriages. Surrey died on the block on 19th January. His father would have followed in a few days only, but the King died instead. It was almost impossible to believe that the great shadow had been removed from England at last.

* * *

They say Henry VIII died muttering 'Monks, monks!' and saw the martyred Carthusians clustering about his bed: called for wine and said 'All is lost', then said no more. Now

Edward VI, aged nine, was King; and my Anthony was in his household. The young King's mother, Jane Seymour, had insinuated herself into Henry VIII's affections so subtly that it had surprised Anne Boleyn on that occasion into labour of a dead boy when she discovered Jane perched on the King's knee. Jane's brothers, Hertford and Lord Thomas, had used the same tactics for some time before the late King's death; as I have said, they were responsible for that of Surrey, and Surrey's old father Norfolk, saved by a single day from the block, retired, defeated meantime, to his estate of Kenninghall and was no more taken heed of for long, until just before his death: he might have said, with Cardinal Wolsey long ago, *If I had served my God as I have served my King, he would not have brought my grey hairs down to dishonour.* Whether the ghosts of Norfolk's two murdered nieces haunted him I cannot say; no one regretted his going, but as I say he was to return, like a ghost himself.

The Protestant Seymours were now in power. Hertford, soon made Duke of Somerset and Lord Protector, held the person of the King, and, to do him justice, used the boy kindly. But he was under the thumb of his wife, a termagant who resented the superior rank of poor Catharine Parr, the Queen Dowager. That last, in love with Lord Thomas Seymour for many years, married him secretly a few weeks after King Henry's death, to the scandal of those who said she should have waited longer; but she had waited long enough. There seemed to be happiness for her at last; Kate said the queen was like a young girl again, and her garden at Chelsea a lovers' paradise. Lord Tom, soon Lord High Admiral of England, was considered a swaggerer, but that was a part of his charm; he had seduced a poor woman seven years back and ruined her, and more of that, or near it, was to come later. Bird of ill omen as I myself now became, I saw doubt in everything; it even seemed to me that Kate, who said she had never misliked the old King—he probably reminded her of my father—would not have minded becoming his seventh wife had anything mischanced to the Queen. They said old Henry had in any case been plotting against Catharine Parr once more before he died, as she continued barren and Kate was not. At any rate, Henry VIII was dead; and his huge coffin burst on the way to Windsor, dripping foetid blood and pus on the ground as it stood by night at Syon on the way. A little bitch dog crept up and licked it, and the folk watching crossed themselves and recalled that it was five years to the day since young Catharine Howard's death on the block on Tower Hill.

The Duchess of course had many suitors now she was a widow and the King's liking no longer a danger to them, as it had been in their time to Anne Boleyn and poor

Northumberland. One of these aspirants was Stanislaus Augustus, King of Poland, who had seen and admired Kate when he was in England in my father's day, perhaps at the very dinner where she took Bishop Gardiner's arm with the gibe I will relate in its place, later. Kate laughed now at the Polish ambassadors, being taken up with her sons, her promotion of the new learning, and the friendship of the remarried Queen Dowager and also the young Princess Elizabeth, who together with little Jane Grey was in Catharine's care. Elizabeth Tudor was a meek young woman with red hair smoothly parted under her round hood, and a habit of looking modestly down, dressing plainly and saying little.

She was present, as were Kate and I, later on, at a notable sermon delivered by a fiery Scots preacher named John Knox, whom the young King had caused to be freed from the French galleys, where Knox had laboured since his suspected part in the murder of Cardinal Beaton in Scotland two years earlier. He was the most thunderous preacher I have ever heard, more so than Latimer, although his bitter jests and earthy humour resembled the last; his glowing eyes were terrible, and he thumped the edge of his high desk as if to knock it to pieces like a madman; possibly his piles were paining him. The young King listened gravely, wearing as always a round hat with a plumed feather, and his Garter. Edward

VI listened a great deal; when he spoke, it was, not surprisingly, about religion, somewhat priggishly as he had been soaked since the beginning in disputations by Cranmer and the like, hearing none other viewpoint. Cranmer himself was to consult this pile-ridden Knox later on about the wording of certain parts of the newly constituted Book of Common Prayer, with the result that the Body of God was itself denied in England, in such fair language that it persuaded many that it spoke truth.

I watched Anthony, with the Duchess's two sons, sit obediently through this sermon. It troubled me that he must hear only such things, and begin to believe them; but I dared not speak. All that happened after the Queen Dowager's matter. Catharine was so much in love with her new husband Tom Seymour that she fell pregnant by him, a thing which as I say had not happened with any of her former three husbands, but all of those were old.

The Queen Dowager was so full of joy that she was like a transported being, and I will say Lord Thomas was the same; both of them made plans together for the coming child and began to amass a rich treasure for it, gold and silver cups, fine linen and the like. The Dowager went very fine herself, wearing a diamond necklace above her pregnancy much as Madge Douglas, whose son had been born and died, had worn her three great brooches with their draped gold chains.

Madge herself, now in the north with Lennox her lord, had given birth since then to a second Lord Darnley, who was said to be handsome, golden-haired and a prodigy of learning. All of these poor children were prodigies.

So matters went, with the Duchess of Somerset aping the manners of queen, and her grave lord doing the best in the difficult task surrounding him on all sides. There began to be gossip about Tom Seymour's conduct as regarded the Princess Elizabeth, although the Dowager was often present when he tickled that young lady in bed of mornings, smacked and played with her, as they reported later. It is said that even then he planned to marry the Princess if his wife should die in childbirth, which poor Catharine Parr in the end did. The child so greatly hoped for was a girl, and my Duchess was asked to house her when her father, Lord Thomas the Admiral, was arrested shortly for treason.

'She lives on,' Kate said with a look of dislike. This poor child of the dead Queen and the Admiral, whom nobody now wanted, lived, while Kate's sons later died. I think that was one reason why Catharine Parr's daughter Mary Seymour was sent north to strangers as soon as might be; as the days passed, the Duchess could not bear the sight of her or contemplate her costs.

Such hopes had preceded Mary's birth; she should have been reared as a princess; but in the end, I heard, she was married without distinction in the northern parts, and no longer in first youth. As for the rich silver cups and other gear she had brought, they did not go with her; nor did a diamond necklace of poor Queen Catharine Parr's, which the Duchess of Somerset kept for herself and which passed to her family. I could have spoken out about all this, but it was not a time to speak, and later on there was small opportunity.

Meantime, Frances's husband Dorset became Duke of Suffolk by reason of his wife's inheritance later. Frances had triumphed, therefore, for the time, and thereafter took no heed of Kate. I heard of this last early by way of Anthony, who came to me in distress. He had inherited my love of animals, and Tom Seymour had tried to force his way into the King's rooms one night to see Edward and beg his protection as the net closed in; the King's little dog, which slept outside his door, barked and raised the alarm, and the Lord High Admiral killed it.

Seymour was shortly beheaded for treason, less because of the King's dog than for other activities, and discovered on his dead body, inside his shoes, was a pair of letters, one to the Princess Elizabeth and another to the Princess Mary. Nobody will ever know the truth of that matter, other than it made forever of Anne Boleyn's daughter a cautious creature with a double tongue; as far as we ourselves were concerned, it meant housing the little baby Mary Seymour at Grimsthorpe, which should not have been any great trouble, but Kate continued to grumble at it and said it cost her money no one would ever repay.

Thomas Kyme, Anne Askew's widower, had meantime sent for his daughter to be returned to him in the north, saying his family was an ancient one and she was not to be made a sempstress. I never heard what became of her.

10

'Were I to marry the King of Poland, Master Latimer, I would miss your wife's churching, and that would be a pity.'

Hugh Latimer screwed up his great hook nose and grinned in his beard, showing yellowed teeth. He was unmarried and remained so, for among the Duchess's dislikes was, curiously, any abandonment of celibacy by the reformed clergy; Cranmer was known to have smuggled his wife across from Germany in a barrel to avoid scandal, and Kate made great mock of him. Now, preacher Latimer replied that he had played the merry-andrew at the friar's roasting long since, but did not disallow the habits of friars; and I stared at the moving folds of his ancient black woollen gown as we walked up and down the garden at Tattershall and thought how he constantly harked back in mockery to that agonised death of John Forrest, years ago now, as if it sustained him in his own estimation of himself. He in fact preferred books to women, so in this as well as the rest he and the Duchess could be friends. As for titles, Latimer had long discarded that of Bishop of Worcester, given him in Anne Boleyn's time when he was her chaplain. He despised all such promotions, papal and other. He believed in the direct message of God to the likes of himself, and expounded that theory again now, his spectacles, without which he found it difficult to see to read, pinned to his gown meantime lest he lose them.

Charles, Anthony and I—Lincoln was still with the King, and the two boys rode at the ring together—had lately returned from our own ride together over the flat, flat land, and had duly tidied ourselves for presentation to Charles's mother. Charles himself walked beside me sedately, his merry face grave; the mention of Poland disturbed him; it was a long way off and he might lose his mother. I assured him in a low voice that she would not be going there; I was wrong, but did not know it yet.

Instead, half my mind was with the south parts, with restless Devon; where the hidden

Catholic faith was still active and no picked bones dangled yet from gibbets. Priests had less hard a time there in the warm air than they did in the bitter Yorkshire dales, living up there exposed to the weather in such rough shelter as they might find and going about their duties with secret devotion and great courage, supported by a few, despite the danger. Hugh Latimer was still talking about Poland.

'Madam, King Stanislas Augustus has had two wives. They say his Italian mother poisoned the last, six months after her coronation. Barbara Radziwill is dead, poor soul, therefore; but you yourself might have fostered, as she did, the flame of the new faith, though you would have been in danger from old Barbara Sforza. It is best to stay at home, therefore, and do what you may in known parts, among your friends.'

I thought of what that meant; the indomitable dark-clad figure of a woman riding back and forth about Lincolnshire, destroying shrines and rood-screens, because the reformers had it that no image should come between God and the common man. Some of these shrines had been very ancient, as might be expected in a country which had been Christian since the days of the early Britons, before even the Romans came. Tattershall church itself suffered, and Her Grace hammered away at the cloisters there till they were gone, saying there should be no more idle walking up and down for monks. In this she had the support of the Bishop of Lincoln, who called himself Holbeach although his true name had been Rands until he became a monk of Croyland formerly. Like many, the abandonment of his true conscience left him open to the assaults of the devil, and made him zealous in a cause of which he should have been ashamed. Lincoln itself had been pillaged already by the old King in his time, much gold and silver taken and many precious stones pried out, and the gold shrine of St. Hugh itself destroyed even as that of St. Thomas of Canterbury had been; but they left the great rose window, broken glass being of no value to them. The Duchess later smashed the statues standing in niches outside Thornton Abbey, and did more damage inside, until they came on a sight which gave even Kate pause, namely the skeleton of a man seated at a table behind a wall, with an open book and a burnt-out candlestick by him. This was the bad fourteenth abbot, Thomas de Fretham, whom it had taken twenty years for the monks to accept in Richard II's time, and who had been walled up later for his sins. Kate quipped back that as de Fretham had been a bad abbot, he should be allowed to rest in peace, and had them replace the bricks in the wall. I did not follow her on these evil forays; it was impossible to stop her, and both Latimer and Bishop Holbeach egged her on in such enterprises, which my father, had he been still alive, would never have allowed her to carry out; nor did the common people like it, for it took longer for the old faith to die in Lincolnshire than in many parts of England, it being deeply rooted there and surviving in secret still. I remember once Kate riding back, full of godliness and grimed with stone dust, being then disturbed by a raven croaking behind her left shoulder. It is an old superstition that this means ill luck, but as the Duchess was out to destroy all superstitions as she claimed, the bird's clamour should hardly have troubled her. I spoke about it later to Richard Cranwell; he had calm explanations for all such things. Ravens, he said, had been painted on the sails of the foraying Northmen when they came to ravage Lincolnshire and the coasts long ago, being considered by them sacred birds because a raven sat forever on each of Odin's shoulders to advise him in wisdom, he being blind of one eye, having plucked it out himself after a promise that if he did so, he would become wiser than any. 'Accordingly, ravens are accursed among us in England to this day, but in truth they are harmless, and will become tame if they are let,' Cranwell said. 'It is true that they are like dogs, and will eat carrion, but men will eat a hung bird or a shin of beef, so where is the difference?' We forgot the raven, at any rate, in other events; but later on I remembered.

*   *   *

At the young King's coronation when he was nine years old, he had worn a light crown in which was set the great sapphire out of Scotland. I remember what Madge in the days of our early friendship had told me about this jewel, whose story she had had from her mother the old Queen of Scots, who would no doubt have the rest from her first husband James IV. It had belonged to the early Kings and had been filched with all the other Scottish regalia by Edward I, and that single jewel had been given back to Queen Joan Beaufort as a bride after having been briefly in the possession of Bruce's renegade son, who was a friend to England's King. Queen Joan later for safety, on her husband James I's murder, sent it south to Cardinal Beaufort her uncle, and so it passed into the hands of the Church and was worn by an archbishop in Edward IV's time, the very time of Warwick the Kingmaker, my great-uncle. According to old Queen Margaret, it was thereafter among the jewels willed to herself by Henry VII her father, to be sent to her in Scotland after his death; but Henry VIII ignored all his sire's other bequests and ignored that likewise. It was not the chief cause of Scotland's entry into the French war, but it helped the matter. The splendid new King Henry, whom men then watched playing tennis because of the boyish rose-flush of his skin, got himself gilded armour and made war on France in order to wear it, and to squander his father's accrued gold in acquiring the Pope's golden rose for obedience. The coffers were soon emptied that Robin Dudley's grandfather, in the time of the old Tudor King, had filled by extortion from the people. The end of it all was Flodden, with the King himself absent in France with my father and Madame, the Queen, Catharine of Aragon, in command at home, and Norfolk and his father at Flodden Field, where James IV and most of his lords perished. All that was long ago by the time of which I write, but soon I had cause to remember.

* * *

Duchess Kate had zeal for her reforming cause and much native wit and beauty, but tact was never one of her attributes. Once I was riding with her past the Tower on our way to visit Frances Dorset at the Minories; Frances had lately made herself pleasant, for whatever reason. It was a fine day, and a prisoner was looking out of his window, as Thomas More had once done for the Carthusians. I saw that it was a face with a drooping left eyelid. Bishop Gardiner, confined lately for his way of preaching before the young King and his advisers, differently from Latimer's homely sermons about colliers and woodcutters and ordinary folk. It was by no means either the style of the thunderers, and evidently made it clear that, although the bishop had in the old King's day been a Henrician, no doubt against his own conscience, he was free these days of that terrible presence and prepared, in time, to become reconciled to see the See of Peter when occasion should offer. This display of courage would not do, and he was clapped in prison.

However he seemed cheerful enough, and doffed his cap to the Duchess as her train clattered by. This was courteous, as Kate had been most uncivil to him at Grimsthorpe in my father's time, when the Bishop came to dinner. 'As I cannot go in with the Duke, whom I like best, I will take your arm whom I like least,' she had remarked then, and now called out clearly, 'It is merry with the lambs now the wolf is shut up.' I knew Gardiner would not forgive this second public insult, any more than the naming of Kate's dog after him. He had heard of that, and the time would, of course, come when he made her pay.

I kept my silence as usual, and we reached Frances in proper course, finding her loud and bullying as usual; little Lady Jane was back with her parents, having been returned from the dead Admiral's house. She and her two sisters were upstairs with their tutor, and we did not see them. The talk ran on the godly marriage, as it was called by the Protestants, which had been proposed for our King with the child Queen of Scots. Frances spoke of that scornfully, as if it would never take place, which in the end it did not; and nobody mentioned the burning and destruction of the abbeys up there, which grave Somerset had accomplished because of the Scots Queen Regent's unwillingness to hand over her daughter. The pillage was far worse than it had been in the old King's time, and left the Borders and Edinburgh in ruin, worse even than Yorkshire after the Pilgrimage of Grace.

Anthony was returned to me about then with measles, much mortified as he should have had them with the rest when he was younger. He had had to withdraw from a fencing-bout with Barnaby Fitzpatrick and young Lord Strange. I liked Anthony to make such friends, who would be of use to him as he grew to manhood; but now was concerned only with his health, for once the rash was over, he continued languid, and had grown very tall while in bed. I feared consumption, and it came to me how I would lose all reason for living if I lost my son. I nursed Anthony faithfully, watching his face day and night; it was grown in feature like Tom's, with the strong nose and cleft chin and clear beautiful jawline I remembered; I thought also of my son's immortal soul, and of how in such company as he daily kept he had never heard any speak of God's love, only the ranters who now ruled England through their eternal sermons; and while Anthony was still confined to bed brought Master Richard Cranwell to him to play chess. This diverted him, and I knew Cranwell would use the opportunity to say certain other things to him, not to bring himself into any danger thereby but to start the boy's thoughts in different ways than had been the custom at Court. I would stay with them at first, then began to leave the two alone as they made the moves in friendly fashion together. It was at this point that Frances invited me with my son to stay at Sheen, to enjoy the summer air out of the city.

As I have said, she had become pleasant, in fact overmuch so, as if anxious to atone for her former lack of graciousness to Kate about the boys' titles. I later found that the reason was, of course, the nearness of Kate herself to the young King by means of her elder son Suffolk, by now Edward's close friend. Frances already had it in her mind that her daughter Jane, stubborn as a mule in reformed doctrine, should become Queen, but not in the way this was in fact attempted later on. Jane Grey, and not the little Queen of Scots, was to become the bride of Edward VI according to Jane's mother. According to Edward, however, he wanted a foreign princess well stuffed and jewelled, so Anthony related to me. The King might have been thinking of Madame Elisabeth of France or again of the Emperor's unknown daughter.

Anthony wandered mostly by himself about the ramshackle old palace and park, for the Grey children were kept close at their books, with tutor Aylmer, winter and summer. My son was not yet quite well, but thank God it was not, after all, consumption, which however the King took about then like so many young male Tudors. Sheen itself had been rechristened Richmond by Henry VII, after himself before he became King, but folk used the old name still. It was about to be rebuilt and much altered, but the rebuilding had not started yet and meantime, Frances and her Dorset were suffered to live on there. I occupied myself with walking among the trees in the park and reading mostly in the house, for Frances bore me little company after the first. One day Anthony came to me white-faced, to say he had found a dead man in the attic.

I rose in alarm, thinking it had happened lately; but Anthony said in a quiet voice—he had grown very quiet in those days—'No, it is coffined, and doth not stink; the body is embalmed.' He knew as much, being apt.

For some reason, I did not go to Frances, as no doubt I should have done, or to Dorset himself, whom I did not like. I picked up my skirts and climbed the stairs with Anthony, and we clambered among the attic rubble until we came on the long coffin, shoved among forgotten things. The lid was loose and Anthony lifted it carefully. Inside lay the dead man with his calm face, long red hair straight to the shoulders, and a deep wound in his throat, the wound's edges having dried and shrunk long since with the embalming and with time. The beauty of the pale dead face astonished me. I made the sign of the cross upon it, and told Anthony to replace the coffin lid; it had been pried open, and that lately; the joints were still bright and there was dust on the corpse. There was a time when he would have scoffed; the reformers do not believe in prayers for the dead. I did not yet know the dead man's name and resolved to find out more by asking elsewhere than from my hosts, who would mock and take no heed. I made Anthony promise to hold his peace and held my own, until I found what I had hoped for at Sheen; a very old servant, so old that he was like a crooked tree; he had been there forty years, for I asked him of it. He remembered the regency of Catharine of Aragon while her husband was in France; it had happened shortly after he took service.

'There was a great victory won over the Scots at the time,' he said. 'The Scots King's body was brought down here, having been killed, they say, a lance's length from the Earl of Surrey, the English commander. There was a great story then. They brought down all the fine French cannon made of brass, I remember, and other loot, but no prisoners.' The silence was ominous; the dim old eyes looked past me at nothing, remembering. 'They say many lords died round him, but more I know not.'

Flodden. That battle had been fought nearly forty years back; and the King's body brought south, a trophy to present to Henry VIII when he returned from France.

'What happened?' I asked. 'Why hath no one buried him? He was a brave enemy; it is not right that he should lie up there, among lumber.'

The old man's eyes slid sideways and he murmured that it was maybe not safe to say. The Pope had excommunicated the Scots King, because he made war on the Pope's allies, England and Venice, and instead aided France, the rebel. As James IV was excommunicate, King Henry, then an obedient son of the Pope, declined to bury him. 'He lay in the chapel while there was a chapel, but now there is none.' The disgust of the thing stuck in my throat and I turned away from the old servant. 'Someone should see to it,' I said. He agreed that someone should, then went away. I spoke of it later to Anthony, explaining what I had discovered.

'That dead man in the attic is James IV, King of Scots, once known for his skills at surgery and poems and the lute,' I said. 'He pinned wings on a man to see if he could fly—the man could not, and broke both his legs—and tried all manner of other things, and was much beloved by his people. At the end, he fell bravely in a war not of his making.' I had all of this from Madge Lennox, who likewise had it from her mother Margaret Tudor, who had herself been first married to James IV in the days when she had been called the Tudor Rose and he the Thistle, and both countries hoped for peace. Anthony looked at me now with his father's eyes, wisely.

'If the late King failed to bury him because he was excommunicate, King Henry was excommunicated also, later,' he said, in the disputatious way they had taught him at the young King's court. 'It is not seemly that anyone should remain unburied. When I return, I will tell the King.'

But other things happened before then.

I did not tell the Dorsets about the King of Scots' unburied body; they may have known of it. Nor did I tell Kate, remembering her bricking up again in Lincolnshire of the bad bishop behind the wall. I went to Richard Cranwell, however, and told him; also that Anthony had made no adverse comment regarding my open sign of the cross, although such things were jeered at now at Court for mummery and Popery and were dangerous. Like Anthony himself, the priest regarded me wisely, saying that, in some manner, he would arrange a quiet burial. He added that it was like enough that Queen Catharine of Aragon, a strict daughter of the Church, had kept the coffin in Sheen chapel until her lord came home from France, then he, full of victory, had put the matter aside meantime for other things. In the end, the body was at last buried, God knows where, but by that time the rebuilding at Sheen had started and inquisitive workmen had cut off the head. We found out later that that had been cast, in the end, on to a cart passing by to collect rubble in Wood Street one early morning. Such things happen; but all our bones will be joined together again at the resurrection on the last day.

* * *

Master Cranwell said Anthony's mind was forming itself in the way we had hoped, but such things must come slowly and I had been right not to speak to him of it. 'The Duchess plans to send her two sons to Cambridge, which is full of the new thought,' he said, and suggested that I send Anthony instead to Oxford, where friends of his own would have an eye to him. I have never been more thankful than that I did so. It was difficult to explain to Kate why this must happen, and although I did not like telling untruths I implied that Tom himself had been at Oxford, which he had not, and that I wanted Anthony to follow in the ways of his father. 'Which college did your Tom attend?' asked Kate in her bright way, and I said with truth that I did not know. She left the matter, talking on cheerfully about how she herself intended to take a house in Cambridge, to be near both her sons. She loved them dearly and craved their constant company, but I myself would not have taken a house to be near Anthony; a boy must become a man in his own fashion, and not cling to his mother or his mother to him. However all of them were still young, even Kate.

The King was young also but no longer in full health; they pretended he had caught a chill while playing tennis. The last time I saw Edward VI ride by he had secret eyes and a pale peaked face, like one who looks inwards and not outwards. I myself think that had he lived to manhood Edward would have become a tyrant like his father, perhaps as treacherous; he signed the death-warrant of his uncle the Protector Somerset, who had been good to him, and Robin Dudley's plausible father gained the Northumberland title and the reins of the realm instead. What followed was not witnessed by us, but I heard of it; the King one day plucked the feathers from his patient hawk till it was naked and said, 'One day I will use you, my lords, in such a manner,' and might well have done so. But he did not; no one knew for certain of what Edward VI died in the end, but of course there was talk of poison; they say the King's hair and nails fell out and so did those of a laundress who washed his linen.

That was however not yet; and Kate and her sons stayed meantime in Cambridge, where Harry Suffolk was said to be a prodigy of learning and Charles not far behind. Certainly both boys were strong, like our father; young Suffolk on a brief visit to France had astonished them there with his horsemanship. There had been much competing also at Court, where the King himself was a fine rider before his illness got the better of him and they all rode often together at the ring. Now, however, the talk was all of Greek and Hebrew and dialectic, with Latin spoken at meals and an erudite treatise written on the Duchess's dead friend, Martin Bucer, the preacher. A fine body and a fine mind are things much to be desired, and I hoped Anthony would achieve as much. He wrote to me diligently, and seemed content. Meantime, as Master Latimer was much in evidence at Grimsthorpe, I accepted an invitation from my kinswoman Lady Margaret Nevill to go and stay with her for a time at Buckden, the place from which my father had once been ordered to go and evict Queen Catharine of Aragon and she had refused; but it was in better order now. Margaret Nevill was also the late Queen

Catharine Parr's stepdaughter, and so I took with me poor little Mary Seymour and her nurse, hoping for an offer of a kinder home than Grimsthorpe for the child; but none came, although Margaret Nevill had known much kindness from the dead Queen while still the wife of Lord Latimer, before the King took her.

Mary was a beautiful little girl, and I could not then understand Kate's aversion to her; perhaps she was afraid the child would become the wife of one of her sons in time, but that I know not. Mary had been taken back, unwelcome there as everywhere, by the time Kate wrote urgently to me to say there was sweating sickness broken out at Cambridge, and would Lady Margaret receive them all three till the threat of it had passed over?

I knew Margaret Nevill would do anything of that kind, for she was avid for Court preferment. I remember I rode out alone to Graffham Water and watched the wind ruffle it, waiting for Kate and the boys to come, and thinking how odd a thing it is that the sweating sickness is said only to attack Englishmen. The pomp of banners and outriders came at last, and I saw Kate's small dark-clad figure in the saddle close beside the tall one of the young Duke, who had grown this past year; he was handsome as a god, Charles less so, but flinging his arms about me and giving me a great hearty kiss. I loved them both, but

Charles reminded me the more strongly still of our father.

'We went to Kingston first,' said Kate in a low voice. 'George Stanley there is dead of the sickness, so we rode on here.' It was a dire thing to say, as though she brought death with her openly; and so it proved. That sickness strikes fast. At supper, the candles burned still and bright; the young Duke was on my right hand, and I remember he gazed at me with a strange sudden look, then turned to his mother.

'O Lord, where shall we sup tomorrow night?' It was like a prophecy; I replied lightly, though my heart sank. 'I trust, my lord, either here or elsewhere at some of your friends' houses,' I said. They had many friends in that countryside, and most others, and rode out often, being made welcome everywhere.

'Nay, we shall never sup together again in this world, be you well assured.' The young Duke began to laugh then; I will never forget that strange laughter, nor yet know its reason. That night after midnight, word came that he was ill. By seven in the morning, he was dead. Harry Suffolk had been the hope of England as well as of his mother. Had he lived, matters might have sped very differently.

Charles Brandon, younger of the name, was Duke of Suffolk for the space of a half-hour. No one had told him of his brother's death, for there had not been time. It was however as though he knew of it; they had always been close. 'Well, my brother is gone, but it maketh no matter, for I will go straight after him,' Charles said. He died within the half-hour. Kate did not see her first son die, but had risen, her hair streaming unbound over her shoulders, to be with the second as he went. She seemed unafraid of the sickness for herself, and so was I. I remember knowing a great thankfulness however that Anthony was at Oxford; then praying for the dead boys' souls, as their mother would not. Even then, Kate was steadfast in her reformed beliefs. She was nevertheless stony with grief. I remember for the first time seeing her as a young Roman matron, showing no emotion at the death of two sons; I tried to go to her to comfort her, but she thrust me gently away.

'It is God's will,' she said, and sent then for her Bible. It was the one Anne Askew had given her in Coverdale's translation, and she brought it everywhere with her, likewise here. I left her reading it, and went to see to the burying of the two dead boys. It would have to be done quickly and without pomp, here at Buckden.

* * *

Afterwards, we returned to Grimsthorpe. Kate had been silent since the deaths, but once we were back home put her arms round me and said, 'Stay with me, Mag,' as my father had asked me to do at the time of his own dying. He might as well never have lived; the marriages might never have been; there were no heirs left. 'Stay with me.' I promised again, and knew I would not break my promise, whatever befell.

The child Mary Seymour, who had taken no sickness, toddled across the grass beyond the window, trailing a plaything and followed by her nurse; they took no heed of Kate.

* * *

I had never greatly taken to Lady Jane Grey, Frances' eldest daughter, although I was sorry for the child, having seen her constantly bandied about between her harsh parents and ambitious guardian, who recognised Jane's nearness to the throne. I also admired her scholarship in Hebrew and other dead tongues I myself have never mastered. However like Kate, Jane Grey had no tact, and unlike Kate was not beautiful, being at that time somewhat spotty due to her age. Otherwise she resembled Princess Mary in stature and somewhat in features, likewise, most assuredly, in stubbornness.

The two did not now deal well, though the Princess had earlier been very fond of Jane. The remark 'Did not the baker make *him*?' made in the hearing of Mary Tudor herself regarding the Blessed Sacrament, is an example of the way Jane spoke downrightly and without regard to the feelings of others. Nevertheless what happened to her next was cruel, and increasingly so until her death, when she duly became a Protestant martyr.

Northumberland kept the fact of King Edward's own death quiet for three days, and would have done so for longer had not the stink of the poor boy's corpse made further concealment impossible. As it was, I heard that they buried it in haste at Greenwich and substituted a more seemly one for a public display at the funeral. This may be true or else not, but meantime Northumberland had prevailed on Jane's father Suffolk, and her half-royal mother Frances, to marry Jane to his own favourite youngest son Lord Guildford Dudley, whether Jane liked it or not. She did not, but her stubborn will was beaten into it, also into acceptance of the crown. Later she was held down by her mother-in-law and husband in order that the marriage might be consummated. Lord Guildford, Robin Dudley's brother—Anthony had known him well at Ashridge with them all—was a biddable enough boy who would have eaten out of Jane's hand, spots or not, had she let him. After they were both arrested he carved her name in the stone of the Tower cell. As for Jane, she was Queen of England for nine days and crowned at Westminster that there might seem to be no doubt, Frances, of all persons, being selected to carry her own daughter's train.

* * *

Meantime, I had a letter from Anthony saying he had left Oxford to join the Earl of Arundel, a strong supporter of Queen Mary. *I name no names, but ask your blessing and your prayers*, he ended; and I knew that Arundel, a bluff man and staunch Catholic, would strike a blow for the true Queen if there was need. Memories were longer in England than the makeshift plotters imagined; the common people had not forgotten Catharine of Aragon and her daughter, or that that daughter was rightful heir of England still. She had allowed herself meantime to be seen by very few, wisely confining her visits to her young brother to special occasions. Now, she showed the spirit of her blood; she took herself to Framlingham, a place of thirteen towers, and raised a thousand men for each tower, by means of her name alone. Then, trustingly, she disbanded all except a body of horse, and without a drop of blood shed rode into London with Arundel and his men by her. Merciful Mary, the people called her then, and I think that left to her own rule she would have remained so, but there were other things. Jane Grey and her husband and father were put in the Tower meantime, but Jane at least was allowed to walk in the garden. Northumberland was executed, but nobody cared for that; the people recalled the death of good Somerset, who had governed well, and one woman thrust a handkerchief stiff with Somerset's blood in Northumberland's face as he was taken to the scaffold. That was all meantime; even Suffolk was spared to betray the Queen later on; and she herself rode through the city in a litter, clad in blue velvet and a jewelled caul so rich and heavy she had to hold her head in her hand. She still had her fierce headaches: the courage of a lion does not drive those away: but Queen Mary had a requiem said in the Tower for her dead brother, which might well rest Edward's Protestant soul somewhat better than the sham funeral. Meantime, I rejoiced for Anthony. Richard Cranwell had told me sometime since that he had been attending Mass secretly for some time near Oxford, where the true Sacrament waited for those who knew where to find it, and had in fact been received into the Church at Stonor. There was no doubt that the old faith might be restored now in England. I was glad of that, but much concerned for Kate, who would not hold her tongue.

11

Any woman must have someone to love, and having lost my father and the two boys, Kate had nobody. I do not mean lesser loves, such as she had for myself, or for the late Queen Catharine Parr, or her friends the reforming preachers at Cambridge, in especial Latimer who was with her as chaplain for nigh on two years, at Grimsthorpe and in London. I mean the kind of love I myself had known, where the man is the only man in the world, the woman the only woman. That love Kate had never met with, for my father had perhaps replaced her own and her fondness for him had been less that of a wife than a daughter. She had loved her sons well, but they were gone. Providence, whom she often quoted, now dispensed for the Duchess of Suffolk what others have had before her age of thirty-three; for the first time, love with a lover. I do not remember when it was that Richard Bertie first came as Kate's gentleman usher, having earlier been in the employment of Wriothesley, except that it must have been before Master Latimer left, for he it was who married them. So discreet were they that I knew nothing of it for some days.

Later on, when it became the concern of certain persons to try to prove that the

Madcap Duchess had not married beneath her on this second occasion, a pedigree was found for Richard Bertie going back to the reign of Ethelred the Redeless, involving an ancestor who had done penance and rebuilt an abbey, others who had ruled a town in Germany in their exile and still been castellans of Dover on return to England and forgiveness. Possibly all of this was true, though at the time Bertie modestly declared himself to be the son of a stonemason. His father had however done well enough to send his son to Trinity, where Richard Bertie had graduated Master of Arts. As far as I was concerned, he was a quiet and scholarly gentleman, reliable in his employment about the Duchess's household, honest, even-tempered and with humour. He was also extremely handsome, tall with somewhat snub features, a fair beard and short hair that curled below his round dark cap, and eyes set obliquely, which gave his face an interesting cast above his long scholar's gown. He was moreover exactly the right age for Kate.

It is difficult to describe quiet happiness, and I will not try to do so; they continued devoted during the troubles Queen Mary endured, the rebellions, her courage and calmness, the bodies swinging from house-doors in London, the final uprising of Wyatt and Courtenay on behalf of the Princess Elizabeth, who like Jane Grey was thereafter confined to the Tower; but, unlike poor Jane, kept her head. Frances had meantime howled at the Queen's feet that her Suffolk would surely die in prison, and the Queen had let him out; promptly, being a fool, he conspired against her in the rebellion, and was taken and this time beheaded. His pickled head was still to be viewed in a church presbytery when I last heard, and Frances had married her young groom of the chamber, Adrian Stokes. I hope the marriage proved as happy as Kate's: it certainly shocked almost as many.

* * *

Kate sent for me shortly, her face radiant. 'I am with child,' she said. 'You are the first to know, except for my husband.' I was glad for her; the tale reminded me somewhat of Job, whose children were restored to him. Nevertheless, I was still troubled for Kate, who was known to have destroyed the shrines and defaced churches in Lincolnshire and to have sheltered Latimer, who was meantime arrested without much delay. He complained of having no fire in prison, but there was fire to come.

Kate sent him money, but was taken up with her new life and heeded his fate less than would have been the case earlier, when Latimer was her sole comfort. Her foe Gardiner was freed again, and high in the Queen's counsels as Bishop of Winchester. I knew that it would not be long before his hand fell on Kate's household; and began to turn over in my mind the notion of myself seeing the Queen. Anthony meantime continued about Lord Arundel, and wrote to me that the Earl's daughter Mary was as apt in Greek as any, pious and very beautiful, with dark hair. It is the only time I have known Anthony to be taken with a young woman, but Mary Fitzalan was soon to be married to dead Surrey's son, to be made the new Duke of Norfolk when his bitter old grandsire should die at last.

* * *

Kate gave birth easily, and this time it proved a girl, whom they named Suzan.

The cup of happiness would have been almost full but for the swinging pendulum of events, and Bishop Gardiner as I say had not forgotten having Kate's dog called after him, and the rest. He was a man who took insults to heart, being unsure of himself, or perhaps anxious to prove himself; it was murmured that he was a bastard of old Jasper Tudor, Earl of Pembroke, and if so such Tudor blood as he had boiled now. He summoned Richard Bertie to Southwark to answer for his wife's opinions. It was no doubt merciful that he did not send for Kate.

She stood to watch her husband ride off, holding Suzan in her arms like any peasant woman might; beneath the dark hood her face was white. 'I may never see him again,' she said quietly. 'We have had so short a time of happiness.'

Bertie raised his hand to her, they all rode off with a clatter of men-at-arms, and we women turned back into the house.

* * *

It was summer, but we had no heart to go out over the next few days; Kate continued languid, staring at the empty hearth. The baby was quiet, smiling and never fractious; she had bright hair, like her father.

To our great relief, some days later Bertie rode back. We had not heard him come, nor yet expected him. He stood in the doorway beaming, still in his riding-coat, and opened his arms to Kate, who ran into them. 'If my clothes stink, it is the Marshalsea,' he said. 'I can say to all that I have spent a night there, after first seeing the Bishop; then he said his prayers, and sent for me again next day.'

Kate was sobbing with gladness; I had never seen her as openly disturbed. She clung to Bertie, asking him all manner of questions quickly, not in her usual calm way; what temper had Gardiner been in, what had he asked, was there yet further danger? Bertie looked grave, put her gently from him, and strode over to where Suzan lay, giving her his finger. 'To answer you in good order, he was surly the first time, but afterwards, I believe, had a good report of me from a serjeant of Chancellor Wriothesley's, who remembered me while I was there.' I recalled Wriothesley as the man who had personally racked Anne Askew, and shut my eyes; neither side was black nor white by now, both being grey. Bertie then said that the Bishop had not commenced with any talk of religion, but only concerning the debts he said my father had owed 'to the King that now dead is'. 'I was able to satisfy him in some detail regarding that, and that the debts were paid long ago,' said Bertie truthfully. 'He said then that he heard much evil regarding religion among us, and asked if my lady wife was as ready now to set up the Mass as she had been to pull it down. He spoke also of the dog.' The dog Gardiner, old now, lay by the baby's cradle; his tail wagged slowly, as if he knew he was spoken about. Bertie said that the Bishop had recalled also the time at dinner at Grimsthorpe when the Duchess had taken his arm as the one she liked least. 'I left that,' said Bertie, 'and stated that, regarding the Mass, divers excellent and worthy men had caused you to abhor it. That, dear heart, is true enough.'

Kate moved towards him and took his hand. 'That was a brave saying,' I put in. Bertie had then gone on to say that if the Duchess should inwardly abhor and outwardly allow, she would show herself a false Christian, 'and, to her prince, a masking subject.' This was true enough, and Cranmer himself had done no less, in the old King's time raising the Host daily, while he abhorred it. 'I said then that one by judgment reformed is worth more than a thousand transformed temporisers.' His eyes twinkled, and I knew he thought of the Cecils, though being a tactful man said naught as they were friends to the Duchess, but had of late become outwardly zealous Papists, though God knows they changed back again as soon as it suited them. For the present, they were waiting for the Prince of Spain to come, early to ingratiate themselves. The Queen's vow to marry Philip the Emperor's son had been the cause of much rioting and rebellion already, but she would by no means change.

I fingered the jewel the Emperor had given me after Tom's death, which lay hidden always in my breast; it came to me that when it was needed, I would take it in gift to the Queen.

'To force a confession of religion by mouth, contrary to that in the heart, worketh damnation,' said Kate. 'Christ himself abhorred hypocrites.'

I asked what the Bishop had said then. Bertie smiled, his face breaking up attractively; I wondered that he had not been married sooner, but no doubt he was waiting for the right wife, or else had been busied with his books and had taken no time to think of one.

'He said,' he remarked, turning to me courteously, 'that that would do well enough if she were coming from an old religion to a new, but that now she was being asked to return from a new to an ancient religion, wherein she used to be as earnest as any.' He regarded his wife quizzically; he knew little of her early days, and would not recall, as I did, the young girl saying her rosary for the Queen-Duchess with us all in the knot-garden at Westhorpe.

'Religion goes not by age but by truth,' remarked Kate. I thought how the truth was older than any scholar; of Christ multiplying the loaves and fishes, of the first Mass at the Last Supper, and how the devil was said even now never to enter bread. The situation by this time was not a mere matter of Popes and princes, of disputing clerics and lay folk; the plain truth was that the nobility of England, my father and Kate among them, had seized abbey lands and would be unlikely to give them back. However I kept my silence. Bertie was still speaking.

'Bishop Gardiner says it will be a marvellous grief to the Prince of Spain when he shall find but two noble personages of the Spanish race in England, and one of them gone from the Faith.'

The other Spaniard, I knew, must be old Inez de Saliñas, the late Lady Willoughby's sister, whom nobody remembered about as a rule and who sat forever at Eresby, mumbling over her beads and praying for her sister's soul and that of Queen Catharine of Aragon. I marvelled that even Bishop Gardiner should trouble to remember Inez, but he had a mind like Thomas Cromwell's, meticulous as to detail; he forgot nothing. 'He let us go, in the end, saying he trusted no fruits of infidelity would be found in you, sweetheart.' Bertie fondled his wife's hand, and Kate answered back with something of her old sparkle that the only fruit so far was Suzan, and then they both turned to their baby and I went out. I was still thinking of the future for us all. Catholic to the heart Gardiner might indeed be, but I did not trust him for himself, nor did I think Kate had heard the last of such matters, despite her husband's apt tongue in her defence.

* * *

At the time of her second marriage, Kate had made over to me, to show her regard and also possibly to rid herself of the burden, the wardship of a young girl named Agnes Woodall who was already in the household. Wardships can be lucrative, although it was not particularly so with Agnes, who was no more than a minor heiress of a Surrey family. In my father's day, he had ventured over far with his wardships, especially in that instance of young Lady Lisle who refused to marry him, and later on of Kate who did not; and there had been young Lord Powis, who was fobbed off, to the fury of his family, with my wanton half-sister by the Duke.

In my own case, this wardship supplemented my income, in addition to what my mother had left and also what was already paid me as the dead boys' governess, much of which last I had saved over the years, for in truth I had little on which to spend money now Anthony was launched for himself. Agnes I will say no more of; she was a furtive child with a habit of picking her nose, and brought me no more pleasure than the Kyme girl had done in her day, but I had some money by way of her, and would shortly require it.

It happened in this way. I was kneeling one morning in my upstairs room in the Barbican house, before the little private altar Tom had bought for me long ago in Brussels. It was old, painted on wood and fashioned of three panels which closed to look like a cupboard for taking on journeys. Opened, it showed the Crucifixion, with our Lady of Sorrows and St. John, and an unknown donor, kneeling. Hidden inside all was a chalice and paten, and when he could do so, Cranwell would come to me daily to say Mass for Tom's soul and my father's.

Now, as I prayed for Tom, there came a scratching at the door; I knew it was not Cranwell, who had already been that day. I rose quickly, closed the altar, turned the key in the lock and hung it again at my belt; then opened the door. Outside stood none other than Master Bertie, tall and grave in his long gown. He had never visited me before. I greeted him civilly and let him in.

He did not seat himself, but stood instead gazing out of the window at the summer's day. He said then 'There will be a fine calm sea,' and I asked if he planned to go sailing. I did not speak entirely in jest, and Bertie took me up with his quick wit; he and the Duchess made excellent partners in all such ways and no doubt every other.

'I am troubled about my wife's safety,' he said roughly. 'Latimer, Bishop Ridley, and Cranmer himself all lie now in the Tower. Kate doth not hide her opinions, and although the Queen would not earlier have punished women, Jane Grey hath lost her head and the princess, they say, may well lose hers.'

'Her Grace will surely not take away a mother from her child. She herself was used so, and will not have forgotten it.' I thought of small Suzan upstairs, of the Pearl of England long ago and Catharine of Aragon, to whom her only daughter had not even been suffered to bid farewell. That had seared Her Grace for all her life, as had the signed betrayal to which she had at last been forced. I thought again of visiting her.

Suzan's father's handsome face was grim

now beneath the round cap. 'Women are no longer protected as weak creatures. Anne Askew was burnt in the late King's time after appalling torture. Cranmer himself burnt the woman Joan Bucer when he had a mind. They blame Her Grace for digging up Martin Bucer's bones. There is vengeance on all sides, merciful as Mary Tudor would once have been. I do not think that it will be better when the Prince of Spain comes. I would take my wife and child out of the country, and I ask your help.'

'What may I do?' I asked him. 'You know I will aid Kate, though you must know well enough that I am not of her persuasion.' I was well aware that Master Bertie was shrewd enough to know of the altar's presence, and of my daily Masses in his wife's house; but I had been permitted them.

'It is this,' he said, his fine scholar's hands—had the stonemason father had such hands, and if not had Bertie got them from his mother, or from the vaunted forebears in the time of Ethelred?—gesturing as he talked. 'The late Duke left many debts in England, those to King Henry having been compounded lately. They arose, as you know, from repayment of the French Queen's dowry, which dogged the couple with debt all through that marriage; and Kate's mother would not permit her daughter's inheritance to be laid hands on for it. Nevertheless if I can persuade the Queen's officers that a pass abroad, for me to come and go, might result in the collection of much money owed to the late Duke by the Emperor, they may well grant leave, and having that permission, I may take away my wife and Suzan till safer times.'

'The Emperor himself is embarrassed for money,' I said, 'and the Fuggers of Antwerp have grown rich as princes on the interest from his loans. He needs money constantly for his wars; I doubt if you would see any.' I remembered the Fuggers riding the streets of the Flemish port in their broad hats of the old fashion, and great gold chains about their shoulders, and outriders alongside them, and much clanking of garnered gold.

Bertie gave a little shrug. 'All of that need not be made known to Bishop Gardiner or the Chancellor, who believe Charles V to be the richest man in the world from his possessions in the Americas,' he said. 'I may say to you, who are wise, that the time I saw the Bishop and he heard me, I spoke of these possible repayments, though I have said nothing yet to Kate. Gardiner brightened in his looks then, but said it would be best to wait till the Queen is married to the Prince of Spain, when he himself will ask Philip concerning it. I put in that it would be best not to act while the Emperor still hath not had his way with England and will do more to placate us, still fearing perhaps that the Queen will marry

Reginald Pole despite his cardinal's hat, and not Philip despite her vow. What do you think, Mistress Blakeborn? You know the Emperor from his youth. Will such a plan as I have set forth serve us?'

'If Gardiner spoke well of it, it hath some chance of success,' I answered cautiously. Bertie laughed, and said, 'He sat back at that and said, "By St. Mary, you speak well".' I reflected that that was the Protestant way of putting the matter; Bishop Gardiner himself would certainly have spoken of the Holy Virgin. Bertie went away, evidently comforted although I had said little. He had without doubt convinced the Bishop at their interview; the pass for him to come and go overseas followed shortly. He departed during that same month of June, and Kate was doleful at his going; neither of us had yet told her the full reason though she may have surmised it. I wrote then, as it was time, to Madge Lennox, who was about Her Grace, to beg permission at last to speak with the Queen privately.

* * *

Word came, and I travelled up by river from the Barbican, finding a litter waiting at last to convey me to St. James's where the Queen went when she had not great business. As I ascended the water-stairs, I saw a thin old man come down to his barge, hunched and with red-rimmed eyes, a cadaver; it was Norfolk, emerged for the last time from his retreat at Kenninghall, and having held the three crowns at Her Grace's coronation, taking the oath with the rest. He wore his Agnus Dei openly again about his neck as he had done at Flodden: it gleamed gold in the fitful sunlight from the river. I marvelled that he should live on, with his son dead as well as so many, and recalled how he had sent to tell the Seymours that they should not take dead Surrey's clothes, as they were stately gear, but should give them instead to the royal children. He did not know me for Charles Brandon's daughter, and gave me no greeting.

And so I came to kneel at last before the first woman to reign in England for four centuries. A small still figure dressed in too-bright silks, her face strained with the late riots so that a frown had furrowed itself permanently between the eyes under the flat coif; a woman brave as a lion, having lately shown the generalship of her grandmother Isabella, the courage and mercy of her mother Catharine, with the latter's stubborn loyalty. Betrayed most cruelly in youth, steadfast since then in her faith despite all threats from men in power, having denied only once in all her life, and to her now undying reproach, under most savage pressure, her mother's rights and her own legitimacy; Mary Tudor, whom I had scarcely seen since she was a young girl playing the lute at Beaulieu, allowed still to know no cares by then, sat here before me in St. James's, her private palace. I remembered Beaulieu as Her Grace bent forward to raise me after my fifth curtsey as prescribed in the royal presences of this dynasty; and was aware of a stench from the Queen's nose. The deep harsh voice spoke pleasantly, however.

'You are Mag, whom our dear Lady Salisbury loved and often spoke of to us. You were with her as she died. We are glad of that. Do you know that her son the Cardinal sent us a poem written at that time by the Lady Vittoria Colonna, when she heard of my own lady's death? *Her limpid spirit is not lost or bound, Nor the invincible legion of her virtues.*' The Queen spoke it in the Italian, knowing I would understand. 'It is so,' I said. 'She is with God, and prays for us.'

'You have kept your faith. We are glad of that also. So many have to be brought back, and they are stiff-necked, like Israel.'

There was no doubt of that, and instead of answering the unanswerable, I drew out the Emperor's jewel from my bosom, where it had lain warm against my heart since the beginning. 'Madam, I have a gift for you,' I said, 'and would ask a favour.'

Her mouth tightened a little. 'Few fail to ask those,' she said. 'You need have brought no gift.' But I turned it towards her so that the deep crystal showed the image clearly, the double portrait of the dead Empress, her bright hair in a close coiled plait, and her young son. The Queen took it in her hands as though it were a relic, and stared at Philip of Spain as a child, and at his mouth.

'I have sworn to marry him,' the Queen said in a low voice, forgetting the royal plural. 'The time was when I would have married his father. You will know that when the Empress died, her son was made by custom to ride with the coffin across Spain, and when they reached Granada, it was opened after many weeks for Philip to say whether or not it was the Empress's body. That was a cruel thing for a boy of twelve; they tell me he fainted. Then, at eighteen, he was widowed of his young wife Maria of Portugal, with whom he had been most happy for two years. I trust to make him so again, if love will serve; for I swear I love him already.'

I said nothing, and presently Her Grace stopped staring at the jewel and raised her head, saying 'What did you want to ask of me?' as if it were of no great moment compared to the other. I asked her quickly if she would spare the Duchess of Suffolk and let her travel safely overseas. 'Madam, she has a young daughter, and she and her husband love one another well. As you hope for such love in your own marriage, have mercy.' I pressed the jewel into her hands; they closed over it, but the Queen still spoke coldly.

'That woman hath done much harm in the eastern counties, destroying holy objects that can never be replaced, and sheltering the heretic Latimer, who jeered at the slow burning of my mother's confessor, John Forrest. Latimer shall burn likewise, I swear, but less slowly; though death is deserved, it need not be so long a torment.'

'Spare the Duchess, madam; she is a woman, as we are. She can do no harm if she is abroad, and out of England.'

Still she was silent, and I suddenly said, 'For the sake of my Lady Salisbury, whom we both have loved, and who should not have died as she did; for her memory's sake, spare young Kate. It is true that she hath made enemies with her sharp tongue; but would you have her dissimulate?'

'No,' the Queen said, 'I prefer honesty. There is little enough to be found.' Her frown deepened, and shortly she put her hand to her head; Madge Lennox, who had remained nearby, came forward. 'Madam, will I burn some lavender in a shovel? That will relieve your head.' The Queen smiled a little, easing the uncertainty that had arisen.

'Madge is a good nurse,' she said, 'but my headaches come and go. Your Duchess may go also, discreetly, to safety; but bid her mind her tongue while she is in England, and tell her I will not free Latimer, trial or none.' The voice was stubborn. I thanked Her Grace, kissed her hands, and left. Madge rode down with me to the water-stairs, passing on the way a tall rough-mannered maid-in-waiting named Magdalen Dacre, who I knew came from the north, and who stared as usual at my malformed hand as she rode towards the palace. Madge said she herself was returning to Syon, where her young son was; and bade me come with her to see Lord Darnley, whom she had named for the late King.

'Harry is a marvel for his age of nine years,' she said. 'He hath written a treatise in Latin for Her Grace, who with all her own knowledge of that tongue greatly admired it.'

Her tone was doting, but I would not go with her to see the pampered golden heir who alone, of all the sons and daughters Madge had borne by then, still lived, and in his later life was to cause great harm in Scotland. I wanted to get back to Kate, in case they had already arrested her, and on my way I wanted to see my Anthony.

The Earl of Arundel was steward of the Queen's household and so my son was here with him in London. I knew that Anthony was sad and pensive still over his love for Arundel's gentle dark-haired daughter, and that nothing could ever come of that; Mary Fitzalan was to marry the handsomest young noble in the kingdom, Norfolk's grandson, now Earl of Surrey in his murdered father's place and soon to be Duke before the year was out. Anthony's love, apt in Greek, would become instead England's premier Duchess, and with her future husband a bastion for the Catholic faith. I did not say as much to my son; he must work such things out in his own mind for himself. I cheered him instead with everyday news of us all, and for my part, left him to go home by water.

I heard later that Madge Lennox had shortly borne another boy, to be named Philip for the Queen's expected Spanish bridegroom. Despite all this, the baby did not thrive any more than the rest. I think there was some disease among these royal persons; all of old Margaret Tudor's first children had died except for James V of Scotland and Madge herself, as well as two whom the old Queen of Scots had borne her third husband after manifesting appetites as varied as those of her brother, Henry VIII. Our own Queen, the sole survivor of her father's own first marriage, had never been healthy; there were her headaches and the ulcer lately inside her nose, no doubt from pox, inherited by way of her father, or that great lecher, her grandfather King Ferdinand, who may have sent it into England with his innocent daughter at her first bridal; God knows. Whatever befell I hoped the Prince of Spain, eleven years the Queen's junior, would make her happy now and would be happy himself. I doubted it, but one must pray.

12

It was raining heavily by the time I got back, as it was to do all that year so that the harvests were ruined. I put off my wet cloak and went to Kate, who as so often these days was striding up and down her solar, ill at ease and defiant. Master Bertie was still abroad, and it was left to me to comfort her, although I did not tell her about the Queen's promise. This would have been indiscreet, as Kate was railing on as usual about the Spanish marriage and how all England hated it, and folk were saying already that there would be no children from it, for nothing could be expected out of the Queen now but a marmot or a puppy-dog. I tried to silence her. 'Do not speak so, for even in your own house you will be heard,' I said. Kate snapped back that she cared nothing.

'To think of good Master Latimer in the Tower, and Archbishop Cranmer also, who never harmed a soul!' she exclaimed. Any harm done by Cranmer I knew to be mostly to himself; his conscience was a pliable thing, and I said so. Kate spat out Philip's name then with venom. '*He* hath said that he would sooner not reign at all than reign over a nation of heretics. That will show you what is coming, the same as what is already, and worse.' Maybe, I thought; and Anne Askew's crazy messages carved in men's minds as though they were stone, though left to die in peace she would have been forgotten soon. I said aloud that Master Bertie could contrive something. The Duchess and Suzan must go abroad for a time, as soon as it could be managed, out of danger. I was cautious concerning this; I did not want Kate to become too openly hopeful, for she could never disguise her feelings. I myself intended to return to England as soon as she and Suzan were safely seen abroad with Richard Bertie, their natural protector. There was no fear for me now as a Catholic, and I wanted to be near Anthony and to welcome, as much as I might, when he arrived, the Prince of Spain; it was possible that he still resembled his portrait as a child, fair of hair, jutting of lower lip; and he would welcome one who knew the Emperor and had also known Madame.

Meantime, matters continued better than they had been in the old King's time, when Protestant and Catholic were latterly taken off to execution in the same cart, and hanged for being one thing and burned for being the other. Now, the Host was again honoured in the palace if not always in the land. I longed greatly to attend the Queen's Masses, which I might do more freely once Kate was gone to safety. Meantime, I honoured my promise to my father to stay with her and keep her from harm.

*   *   *

The escape of the Duchess of Suffolk when it came was considered a triumph by the Protestant party, and few knew that the Queen herself was aware of it and had countenanced it, by my request. Bertie sent word soon that he would be ready with a place on board ship at Gravesend, and would be waiting; meantime, there would be a boat paid for to take us down river. We must get ourselves there in disguise, however, and on foot, early in the morning.

The day we departed it was dense with fog. I could remember Kate as I always liked to do, attired in Court dress for the portrait by Master Holbein in my father's lifetime, before that painter died of the London plague. Then, her smooth hair had been gold-dusted under the new flat coif, her black surcoat edged with pale fur to frame her face, her shift needle-stroked into delicate frills beneath. Now, she was attired in a dark round gown with a gathered linen collar and plain hat, like any merchant's wife or common woman, in order not to be noted on the journey. It was strange to Kate to walk the streets, and we had to surround her to guide her on the way. We were a curiously assorted collection of persons, Cranwell leading; a Greek groom, a joiner who was attached to the household and who might be of use aboard the ship when we got there;

the Duchess's fool she would never part with; a man who could brew ale, and the cook, likewise the laundress. I was carrying little Suzan, who was hardly awake at that early hour. I felt her warm weight close against me.

Immediately we had all stolen one after the other out of the house, things began to go wrong. Despite our care the fool stumbled, waking Atkinson, the Duchess's herald who was not in the secret. He came bustling out, carrying a torch he had lit. The nursing of the flame gave us time to get to the gate, and Kate hurried on without her servants, these having been bidden to make their way to Lion Quay. Meantime, with the herald's alarm, she herself had dropped the child's clothes and the milk-pot she had been carrying, and she, I and Suzan slipped into the shadow of the Garter House next door. We saw herald Atkinson come out, peer round, see only the departing few in the fog, and go back to poke and interfere as best he could with the dropped packages. 'God knows I have never walked streets in my life,' muttered Kate, for as a great lady she had always ridden; and as for Lion Quay, we had lost its direction and had never been there in our lives. However Cranwell, doubling back, led us the right way, without which we might never have reached it, being unable to see a foot in front of ourselves.

We went by Finsbury Fields, and more by luck than good guidance met the others again, for the fog had thickened as we neared the river. By following the wall at Moorgate, we gained the quay at last; we could barely see the boat and the bargeman waiting. He, by then, was unwilling to put out until the air should clear, for the river was crowded with unseen craft that dared not move. 'No, you must set out now,' said Kate clearly and lest he question such high orders from the merchant's wife she was supposed to be, I quietly handed him silver from my own purse. In the end we knew London Bridge to vanish at last in the gloom above us, as we moved down-river cautiously; but could see nothing still except great shapes of coal-boats and looming dark barges.

I too was anxious that the boatman should make haste, despite the risk there was of collision; by now, our flight would be discovered, officious persons would be searching the Barbican house and no doubt taking inventories and setting seals, with perhaps a watch to apprehend the Duchess of Suffolk.

Little Suzan began to shiver on the long dank journey; I rubbed her limbs to comfort her. By the time we reached Gravesend at last we were chilled to the bone, and it was evident that we were expected, for there was a small crowd at the quay, some of whom stared curiously. Cranwell was magnificent, and dissembled all questions, saying only that this was Mistress White, daughter of the merchant to whose house we presently went.

Everything had been arranged in this way, and the unknown daughter existed. Kate did her best to look as she ought, and contrived it by staring at the ground. Presently, Master Bertie was found waiting, and their embrace was a joy I dared not watch, having no longer such joy of my own, but glad for them at their reunion.

The merchant, whose name was Gosling, warmed us with wine, of which we were thankful; and entertained us in his house for a day or two. Kate and I set ourselves to sew new clothes for Suzan, the child's others having been lost at the Barbican gate; and soon enough there came news of our ship, seen to be nearing. There were still perils, though, from folk who thought themselves doing good to the Queen's officers; at the inn where we lay that night there was further enquiry, and again Cranwell came to the rescue, telling the searchers I know not what; by then, I was resigned to the will of God. Thankfully, next day we boarded the ship, the weather having cleared; but there was still the hazard of tides. There were storms also, and twice we were blown back toward England. The second time there were again enquiries from officers, and Bertie and Cranwell, who had gone ashore for fresh supplies, assured them there was only a mean merchant's wife aboard; by then, tossed and seasick as we were, without clean linen meantime, we looked worth less than that, and they were satisfied.

At last it was not, for the third time, Zealand, but the flat lands of Brabant. We landed and got our clothes changed after long; and it was comical to see us as we were meantime, in such hoods as are worn by the local women to hide their faces; but we still greatly needed the disguise. This was Protestant country and we were on the whole safe enough, however, so we took horse then to Cleveland, where Master Bertie had taken a house ready at Santon, it being necessary for him to deal further with the magistrates later on at Wesel, which is itself a Hansa town dealing with the London steelyards. The place we were in was full of folk who had fled the Catholic reign at present in Flanders; I heard much talk against the Emperor and his son Philip, but kept silence.

It may be asked why I did not leave Kate then, as she was safe with her husband, and return to England as I had planned. The reason was that she clung to me and said that she was certainly again with child.

'It happened at the inn in Gravesend,' she admitted. 'I was not sure whether my sickness was for that, or the sea.' She smiled, and I knew that she was happy; but promised not to leave her till the child was safely born, no doubt in a strange land. Bertie himself was glad, and as always, cherished her.

*   *   *

Thereafter, we had more adventures. Our stay in Santon was made uneasy, but there was a friend of the Duchess's there from London who called himself by two names, as many had to; one name was Perusell, the other Rivers. This man was a minister of the reformed religion, and he promised to ensure our safe stay as far as he might.

What followed may have been my fault, for I had written to Anthony to tell him where I was, and he never received the letter. However it might have happened, a bruit got up in the town that we were persons of importance and not what we seemed. Also, though Master Cranwell's demeanour was always prudent, somebody may have guessed that he was carrying mass-gear. He departed finally back to England and I was sorry to see him go; it left me without close comfort in my religion. The rest had gone also, though not the fool, who stayed, and diverted the Duchess through everything. The town's chief magistrate, a Catholic, had been privately informed by Master Bertie of his wife's state, but no one else knew of it except myself. I endeavoured to guard Kate from all petty annoyance, but did not succeed, as I will relate hereafter.

In some manner—nobody is ever certain how such things make themselves manifest—

word had reached Cardinal de Granvelle, the Emperor's legate, of our presence. An order came shortly that the Duchess and her husband were to be examined concerning their beliefs.

This meant danger. There was no hope of sending word to England in time; a man of the town warned Richard Bertie, and he himself came quickly to us and said we must all be gone, taking Suzan up in his arms to cheer her; children feel it quickly when matters are not as they should be, and her mouth had drooped. I packed a few things hastily, and we set out, as we had formerly done, on foot to attract the less attention. Kate was by then growing heavy with child, but carried her husband's rapier and cloak.

It was then February. The fogs of London had been bad enough; now, in the most wicked of months anywhere, there was frozen rain of a kind that can only come from the sea. We walked a mile or more, soaked to the skin, and then the icy cold began to thaw, which meant the roads were no longer hard but rutted, abounding in piled slush. No carriages were to be hired in any village through which we passed, or horses either. Suzan's father carried her all the way. We struggled forward and reached Wesel at last in some fashion; by then it was night. Our Lady and St. Joseph surely met with no worse welcome at the various inns of Bethlehem than we had; owing to our bedraggled appearance it was thought that Bertie himself was a common soldier and the Duchess his woman. What they may have thought I was by then, God knows. Suzan, who seldom caused any trouble, was crying with the wet and cold. Duchess Kate, for that and weariness, was in tears herself. The rain continued to pour down without mercy, as if the heavens had opened.

'By God, we will make shift if needs in the church porch, and I will find coals to light a fire,' Richard Bertie swore. He said also that he would find straw to lie on, and food to eat, for we had had none all of that day. However his intentions, good as they were, proved of no avail; he could not speak the tongue of those parts, and no one knew any English. In the end, we had to thank God for our Latin, which as I say is a language understood everywhere by those who have been to school, and two youths passed by talking it. 'Take us to some Walloon house, and I will give you a stiver apiece,' Bertie managed to convey; and they knew where to find such a place. By this sign, God was certainly with us; I had not forgotten my prayers on the way. The house to which the boys led us chanced to be the very one where our friend the Santon magistrate was having supper as a guest, having ridden over earlier. They had in fact been discussing us and the Duchess's situation. The host hurried out at last in response to Master Bertie's message to a servant, and sure enough there followed Perusell or else Rivers, his hands raised in horror at our state.

Joyful greetings were kept for later; we were taken in, drowned rats as we were, dried, fed and clad in gear belonging to the house's inmates, the host and his wife and child. Suzan, having taken no harm with all of it, fell asleep.

*   *   *

It is from that that the mistaken tale arose that the Duchess of Suffolk had given birth to her son Peregrine in a church porch. In fact it was not quite time, though near it. Master Bertie hired a house in Wesel close by the river, and far from continuing to pretend that we were nobody, it was evidently time to make it clear that we were somebody. That Sunday, I believe, the local preachers inveighed against the inhospitable innkeepers to their congregations. Princes, they said, are received as private persons, and angels in the shape of men; which last was perhaps flattering us a little. One preacher wished his hearers the afflicted hearts of strangers in a strange land, and a broadsheet was shortly issued showing Bertie rebuking the sexton of the church for speaking rudely to the Duchess, the man being given eight tongues of blood spurting from his head, like the flames of Pentecost. Peregrine

Bertie was in fact born comfortably in the hired house in Wesel, his mother having an easy labour as she always did. They named him thus because of the travels, which were not yet done by any means. He was christened in the church of St. Willibrod, though not born there. I was glad of the sight of Kate again with a fine boy in her arms. I prayed that Peregrine might grow up to comfort her for the loss of the other two. The baby was Spanish in appearance, having the oblique eyes of his father seen under dark clear brows. Like the two dead boys, he was strong and muscular. I marvelled that Kate's little body had endured all it and without harm to herself or him, but there seemed to be none, and Peregrine Bertie thrived.

*　　*　　*

We were happy enough in Wesel, and safe for the time. I had written again from there to Anthony, and he sent us news in course. His dark-haired Mary was married and a Duchess, for old Norfolk was dead at last; and was already expecting a child. Anthony wrote of this without comment, as though he spoke of a stranger. He also asked us if the rumour was true that the Emperor had detained Cardinal Pole in a German prison—it turned out to be a monastery—till the marriage of Philip and Queen Mary should become a fact; evidently the Countess's son was still considered a dangerous rival. In a later letter, however, Anthony told us of the Queen's marriage safely accomplished; Philip, made King of Naples in time by his father in order that his rank might not be less than his wife's, had arrived in England in a downpour of summer rain; but the marriage itself, at Winchester, had been splendid, in white, silver and gold with great diamonds, *but the Queen spoilt her dress with a black scarf and scarlet shoes.* Bishop Gardiner had conducted the ceremony, Cranmer himself being in gaol; otherwise, the Spaniards had complained that the bride had no eyebrows and was not as handsome as they had been led to expect. Madge Lennox had attended her.

*   *   *

That had happened some time since, as letters were as a rule delayed. It was from the Duchess that I learnt other news, as late as November.

I found her in tears. 'Good Master Latimer is burnt at the stake, and Bishop Ridley with him, at Oxford in a ditch. Do you know what my dear friend said as the flames reached him? *This day, my masters, we will light such a candle as shall never be put out.* It is true; they are martyrs, and will be remembered as long as there are men on earth.'

I remembered only the roasting friar. There was less heard of John Forrest later on than of the famous burning of Latimer and Ridley; the latter had been much beloved for his charities. I could only close my eyes at the thought of such deaths and be thankful that we ourselves were out of England. I loved the Duchess's children too well by now to return for the time, especially as there soon came other news from Anthony that he was this side the water.

13

I have said that we were happy enough at Wesel, and this is true, though Kate had grown somewhat acid of tongue now that she thought herself secure again. She still had letters from England, and took pleasure in relating to me the failure of the royal marriage, which was becoming increasingly evident although King Philip always treated his elderly wife with courtesy. 'She hath made a fool of him twice now with the rumours of pregnancy, when it can be nothing but wind,' said Kate cruelly; in fact, it was more, as is found in certain high-bred animals or in barren women too greatly anxious for a child; they swell up and their periods cease, and only with time is it proved that no life lies within them at all. Enough cruelty had been the lot of Mary Tudor without that, and it happened to her again the second time after the King's return briefly to England, where he had formerly been for over a year. Meanwhile, Kate related with relish that Philip was now said to be fornicating with a baker's daughter and had thrust his hand in at a window in Hampton Court to try to fondle Magdalen Dacre's breasts, but Magdalen had whacked his hand with a stout stick. The last story was probable, being like Magdalen; but I was sorry for the Queen. My true sadness however was for my son Anthony. On the day the King departed for the Low Countries for the last time, there was the grand christening of young Mary Norfolk's son Philip Howard. Duchess Mary herself lay gravely ill of childbed fever, and shortly died. Anthony wrote to me from St. Quentin, where he had begged Her Grace to send him with letters for her absent husband and permission to remain and fight in Philip's wars.

* * *

I did not know whether my son by now was alive or dead; appalling stories came to us of the battle, also the siege, rape and pillage in Flemish towns, the cruelties of the Spanish and Austrian troops and the suffering of the common people, especially the women. I remembered my former friends in Antwerp and hoped they were safe; no letters could get through.

To relieve my mind, I used to take Peregrine, who walked by now, and his sister down to watch the Rhine flow smoothly between high rocks, and tell them its legends which I had learned long ago from Madame. Suzan asked one day 'What is a mountain?' and I became aware that these children had never seen one, only the flat lands where we lived. I remembered the brown hills in Yorkshire where I had sat with Tom, and described those; but they were nothing compared with what was to come.

* * *

One day, as we sat all three on a flat bank above the water, the Duchess's fool came running, her round face agape. 'There's word from England, mistress, and you're to come, she says quickly.'

I hastened with the children back to the house, one clutching either hand; Suzan's grey worsted skirts bobbed as we hurried, lagging nevertheless because of Peregrine, who was too heavy and manful by now to be carried. I found the Duchess pacing up and down in her old way, and she whirled about to face us. 'I thought you would never come,' she said. 'My husband has had word from the Queen's ambassador, Sir John Mason. It is evident that my Lord Paget's visit to us the other day was feigned to be goodwill only, and that we are again in danger.'

'Why, from whom?' I asked. I recalled Lord Paget as a stout and seemingly harmless personage who had ridden in on his way to the nearby baths for his health. Kate's words came tumbling out quickly, and she gestured nervously with her hands, on which my father's ring and Bertie's both gleamed together.

'King Philip hath left Queen Mary for the war in the Low Countries and will not return. Now the Duke of Brunswick is to pass by here with ten ensigns, and take us prisoner. He is in the service of Austria against the French King.'

That might well be true, as I knew; old Francis Foxnose, the late King of France who had long ago tried to ravish my poor Queen-Duchess while in her white dule, had been no friend to the Huguenots and neither was his son and successor, Henri II. Nevertheless, the Emperor and King Philip were now against France, so religion counted nothing.

The stir in the Low Countries was like an evil porridge; it splashed out on us even here, and those in Philip's employ might well harm the Protestant Duchess, who by now was famous for her opinions.

Master Bertie came in then, his handsome face grave above its beard. 'The Palsgrave hath written, Kate, that he will house us at Windesheim in High Dutchland. That is a refuge at least; best make haste.' He kept in touch with many such persons for the sake of his wife; alone, he might have been left in peace. Kate pursed her lips; she had not forgotten the journey here in February rain two years since, with herself pregnant; but there was no such hindrance now, only the children would need a cart in which to travel.

I cheered as we made ready in all such ways, reminding her that this Palsgrave's brother had in his lifetime been in England in Queen Catharine Parr's time, as a suitor to the Princess Mary whom the Queen often afterwards twitted about him, though the marriage had come to nothing. 'We will not be among strangers,' I said, 'for some will remember the Court. Heidelberg they say is very beautiful, and there is a new university there.' Whether I thought we would sojourn in Heidelberg till Peregrine was old enough to go to the university, I know not; but Kate had used to enjoy entertaining the masters and dons at Cambridge, and might do so again. 'But what are we to live on?' she demanded, which was a practical question enough. Apart from my father's known debts in Europe, some of which had been safely collected by Master Bertie, there was nothing for Kate and her family and servants to live on other than meanly for their state, though I provided my share; her properties in England had been sequestered by the Queen's officers when she left.

'You will meet Melanchthon,' I said, not answering the question about money. 'You can talk together of Master Holbein, who painted you both.'

She took comfort, and said she knew Duke Otto Henry had appointed the great scholar as professor there, 'and there is, they say, a great library, full of manuscripts from Paris and Italy and far parts.' We finished our packing, for there was less gear than before, and had gone before the Duke of Brunswick and his ensigns could ride in with the order to take us.

* * *

This time we were not on foot, but in wagons, and the weather was fair. I will not describe our passing beyond the Low Countries, eastward into the mountains of Thuringia; the children gazed in amazement at the mighty peaks, the tall firs, the stars at sunset seeming as if they were strung like lamps along the sky-high edges. We passed by Gotha, where I was comforted to remember that the Superintendent there had said long ago, after a visit to England, that the Gospel according to Harry was evidently plunder and riches; it showed a right way of thinking. So we came at last to Windesheim; but we were no longer persons of importance, and much in debt, though our host did his best to honour us at his own expense. There was a personage in

Strasbourg, to which place Master Bertie was called one time to arbitrate; this was none other than that same Master John Knox, the Scot, who had so deleterious a hand in aiding Cranmer to reform the Prayer Book to the disadvantage of the Real Presence. I did not want to see him, but Bertie described him as full of fire and zeal, which one could imagine; such persons look on themselves as the direct instruments of God, and nothing will quiet them. He was, of course, safely out of England while Mary was Queen; it was different for him from the time of her brother. I will say little of Windesheim, as it was evident by then that we were poor persons; my own money had not arrived, and Melanchthon did us little good. Luckily our plight was known, and soon courtesy was offered us from still further off. The Palatine of Vilna was none other than Prince Nicholas Radziwill, brother of Barbara, the reforming beauty said to have been poisoned by her mother-in-law after her Polish crowning.

* * *

We were by now so deep inland that no country seemed as far away as England, and it did not matter where we went; in due course, King Stanislaus Augustus himself, Kate's old suitor who had heard of her situation from his brother-in-law, offered not only permanent shelter but a province to rule, as Master Bertie's prudence deserved. It was not large, and the rumour of it resembled that of the fabled Bertie ancestry itself, growing as it rolled; but we had no choice but to accept gladly, and travelled on, thankful to be no longer an embarrassment to our late host.

* * *

It was April of 1557 when we journeyed at last towards Frankfurt. Behind us was war, its shadow ever more terrible and increasing; before us, on the road, gambolled a little spaniel Master Bertie had, which diverted the children. However, there was trouble even because of that; a landgrave rode by with his train, coveted the dog and set upon us, making the children cry as he seized it. He had a great number of horsemen and they proved rough. They rode forward and thrust their spears through the carts where we, the women with the children, were; I hid Suzan's face in my cloak. Master Bertie had but four mounted men with him, yet nevertheless managed by valour to slay the captain's horse under him; and this aroused the peasants, who were told that we were Walloons. They came pouring out of their houses, waving staves and whatever else they might muster. Duchess Kate signalled urgently to her husband to be gone, and save himself on horseback in some nearby town. 'We will shift for ourselves,' she called out, and it was true; with the men gone, we would be safer from attack, of one kind at any rate; God only knew about the other.

But Master Bertie, spurring off, did not fare so well in the town after all, for they pressed upon him there, and drove him up a ladder to a window to save himself from murder, vaulting over the sill, and defending himself with his rapier and dagger from inside the house. Soon the burgomaster was sent for and could fortunately speak Latin, likewise a magistrate who was with him; and Bertie submitted himself to the law, knowing he had done no harm to the landgrave except for killing his horse. He asked for safe-conduct from the anger of the crowd, then gave himself up, yielding his sword at last.

By then, we in our wagon were trundled by order towards the town. We did not see Bertie all of that night, and the Duchess was greatly in fear for her husband; but I bade her be of good comfort. 'There is nothing of which he is guilty, save the death of a horse,' I assured her, nevertheless thinking of the poor brute lying dead with its guts out all over the road; to what straits had we come!

Bertie had evidently availed himself, during his night in prison, of quills and paper, and had written letters, which turned out to be of use, to various lords and landgraves thereabouts. My lord of Erpach, who dwelt only eight miles away, got his by next morning and came at once, knowing already who the Duchess was; and seeing him bow and scrape before her humbly, the hostile crowds melted away, to our great relief; they had remained all night growling and menacing about our cart, and little Peregrine had had to wet himself perforce in the wagon, a thing nobody afterwards liked to remind him of.

Thereafter, with help from my lord, we proceeded towards Poland; and that is not a short journey, nor is the country like any other I have ever seen. For one thing, for the time being at least, Lutherans, Protestants and Catholics dwelt in peace there side by side; and why should they not?

*   *   *

I will mention here a letter I should have received much earlier, but which had been delayed for over a year and found at Wesel lying at last in the empty house. It was a miracle I received it in the end, at a place named Crozan in Poland. It was not from my son, from whom I had still heard nothing, but from Master Cranwell in England. He wished me well, and told me how Reginald Pole, freed at last by the Emperor, had been sent by the Pope to receive England again into the Holy See. Cardinal Pole had travelled up the Thames to Whitehall by water, watched by great crowds, in a barge bearing a great silver crucifix at the prow. *He hath grown a great spade beard, which makes him strange,* Cranwell wrote.

King Philip had met him at the water-stairs, and the Queen inside the palace; and I would have given much to witness the reunion of those two, who might once have been lovers and have become in the end husband and wife. As for England, there was no great welcome for the Cardinal by now, ordinary folk having grown long since bewildered as to what pertained to whom, and although the bishops and clergy duly sank to their knees to receive the Pope's pardon, it was as some matter granted by a foreigner from a foreign state; Pole had been too long away, but would have lost his head had he stayed. He had no choice. That was all the letter said, for it had been written before the King left for the Netherlandish war; otherwise I heard that the Queen herself was in misery with her wretched health, and spent her time sitting on the floor in her apartments, her knees above her head.

Later, after Philip went, it was Reginald Pole who comforted her, and Pole for whom she sent daily from Lambeth across the water, so that men saw his barge come and go. Of that I heard nothing till much later, or that Pole himself was to die on the same day as the Queen; it was as though their lives and their cause flickered out together, for there had been too many burnings by then, including Cranmer's.

*   *   *

Meantime, our own travels continued. We no longer resembled a train of nomads quite so greatly after leaving Frankfurt for the mountains, and crossing the flat Brandenburg plain; we had been met by a clattering noble escort, plumes nodding in their round yellow hats, well armed and mounted on the short-legged white ponies they commonly use in battle. The reason for all this was not our manners or appearance; even my wardship of Agnes in England had been long taken away, no doubt by some clerk who thought he obeyed orders, and I was as poor as the rest. The Duchess and Bertie, though not in debt to anyone, were down to their last penny and almost their last rag, and were shabby, like the two poor children. I looked at Kate and watched the lines deepen about her mouth that had come there long ago with the death of my father's young sons by her; and the mouth itself had begun to grow hard and wry, like an older woman's. Nevertheless, she was still beautiful, and Bertie continued her tender guard and unwearying protector.

It was Kate, not he, who had suggested sending the last of the Duchess's jewels to Stanislaus Augustus, King of Poland, by the trustiest messenger she could find; no less than Dr. Barlow the reformer, who had, like Latimer in his day, been an English Bishop. It was as though to make clear that no beggar was coming to King Stanislaus' realm, but a woman of rank almost equal to his own.

* * *

She was acquainted with a number of nobles from far countries, which would not in fact have been difficult to achieve; there are a great many of them, as it is not the same as in England, where only the eldest son inherits a title; in Poland they all do, but it hardly counts, as the estates are so vast there is room for everyone. One of these persons was called John Alasco, and he had been in England and had studied under the great Erasmus. 'They have one of that master's pupils there now, who hath translated the *De Republica Emendana*,' stated Kate cheerfully, adding with ease that this man's name was Frycz-Modrewski. I listened above the eternal jogging of the escort's hooves. I was not attending closely, because word had reached me that the great Emperor Charles V was dead. He had by the end given up all honours, and had retired to a monastery in Spain, where however he ate melons and other things he enjoyed and led a restful life, without penance. He was proud of the young son borne him recently by a waiting-woman, a boy whom they called Don John of Austria and who was said to be extremely handsome, like his grandfather Philip. Philip the Handsome's widow, Queen Juana of Castile, died then also in her prison; she had been confined for almost fifty years. I remembered again her beautiful face in the Flemish portrait, above the many-coloured cloak, and her long dark hair.

The children slept exhausted in the saddle, carried by servants. Suzan in particular looked white and thin. I think I knew by then that I remained for their sake by now rather than Kate's; my father would have agreed that she lacked nothing, having Richard Bertie. It would be better for Suzan and Peregrine to be settled in one place, however strange, than to continue travelling eternally like gypsies through foreign lands. If Stanislaus Augustus continued to favour us, well and good; the yellow-hatted escort clattered on bravely.

* * *

It seemed an interminable journey, nevertheless; past field after long tilled field, with workers bent double over their hoes till dusk, and we rode on; great remote castles where we sometimes stayed, new mansions that had arisen, prosperous and solitary in their parks; lakes and forests, of a size I had never known; and, always, immense hospitality, which was welcome though we could not speak a word to our hosts or they to us. The language was strange and I was too old by then to pick it up, as I might have done readily in the days of Madame.

At last we came to the town and castle of Wawel, and were taken to the King. He was a man with a big handsome face devoid of life, dressed magnificently in a long brocade robe and furs. He kissed Kate's hands and looked at her intently with his sad eyes. He had been a widower now for five years, and had no son; handsome little Peregrine caught his eye, and I thought how Henry VIII would no doubt have acted in the circumstances, causing Master Bertie to be swiftly removed soon; but here he was safe. The King took the Duchess by the hand and the rest of us followed; he led us round the great new tapestries of which he was proud, with their scenes of trees and fruit and leopards and other animals crouching below. The castle itself was splendid, largely rebuilt by this King, in especial the chapel where his father, the first Stanislaus, who had reigned for very many years, lay now in effigy, his long thin beard trailing over his stony chest. Of the poisoned Queen Barbara there was no sign, except for the sorrow ingrained in the King's face; they had only had three years of marriage, and he had loved her.

'I am the last of the Jagellions,' he said now wistfully. 'When I die, I do not know what will become of Poland.'

'You have done what you can,' said Kate. They spoke in Italian, the language of the King's mother. 'The fields are well tilled, and there is much building.'

The tired eyes lit up. 'You understand,' Stanislaus said eagerly. 'Here a man is either rich or poor, noble or serf; it is not like your England. It is therefore the duty of the nobles to govern their estates well, but not all do so, especially on the border.'

'There is always war on a border; we are the same ourselves, though small. The Scots and English have never agreed, and never will; their minds are different.'

Stanislaus looked at Richard Bertie, standing silent, his eyes on Kate. 'From what they tell me, you are both of you good landlords at home. You husband your estates and are careful of the welfare of your tenants. It is only a step from there to governing a province.' He had been told nothing, evidently, of Kate's throwing down of the Lincolnshire shrines, or perhaps because of Barbara's views he approved of it. 'Would you consider taking charge of a part of the country near my brother-in-law, on the borders of Lithuania? You would be responsible to nobody but myself. I would not make this offer to any stranger who came; but I have heard of your wisdom and discretion, both man and wife, and also your learning. Our scholars speak well of you.'

Kate and her husband knelt, having first smiled at one another; and thanked the King from the bottom of their hearts. I knelt behind, staring meantime at a carved satyr on the ceiling. With this secure place offered her, Kate would not need my services for ever; I could perhaps consider returning home whether or not Anthony still lived, to the land and people I knew. But would the Queen herself live long, and if not, how would matters speed as regarded Rome, and might I openly practise my faith in a new reign in England? I must wait for a little, till there was certain word; and watch Suzan and Peregrine grow up as noble Polish children, Suzan perhaps to marry in that country, the boy to serve its King. As for Kate, she might well live out her life here, managing her province as she had managed Grimsthorpe, with Bertie's help; as long as God allowed, he would remain with her. One must wait.

'My husband and I will do our utmost to be worthy of Your Serene Majesty's trust,' Kate said meantime. Stanislaus raised her to her small height, and once more kissed her hands. He did not, naturally, kiss mine. It is doubtful if he had noticed me.

14

We lived in a red castle in Crozan, from which Kate and her husband governed Samogitia, much as they had governed Grimsthorpe, and I governed the two young children, as I had done the others. I was no longer active enough to ride out daily with Peregrine and Suzan over the flat grey lands, as I had done with Charles and his dead brother in the green England I remembered. Nor would Peregrine ever have learning stuffed into his head as the two dead Suffolk boys had done; he was strong in his body and resolute in his mind, and would make more of a soldier by the end than a scholar. All of us, even I myself, picked up a few words of Polish in the north-east dialect, but most of the talk had to be in Latin, even to our two servants who were both of them called George.

Now and again, we had our diversions; we were visited by our old friend Prince Nicholas Radziwill, and often visited him in return, as he had a high regard for Bertie and his Duchess. In the glorious ancient palace I gazed at last on the portrayed face of his dead sister, Barbara, Queen of Poland. She had been very beautiful.

Barbara need not have died as she did; there was no religious strife. Under Stanislaus

Augustus every man might think and speak as he liked, a state which has not yet been attained in any other country as far as I know; in Geneva, the punishments are more strict than in Rome. At Crozan, on the other hand, I myself could go freely to Mass in the Castle chapel, and in the Duchess's apartments of an evening, when there was talk, every variety of opinion was to be heard, Lutheran, Catholic, anti-Trinitarian, even once that of a Huguenot who had wandered there from France. I can recall the cold dawns coming up from the Baltic while they all talked and talked round Kate's lit brazier, and she herself, sewing by the light of quarrier-candles, worked away at a cushion set with pearls in close embroidery, and now and again lifted her head with some sharp apt saying.

Talk rose and fell, the scholars in their dark caps, the nobles and gentry in furs and brocade, the wine flowing. There were always more men than women present; Kate, whose body was most womanly, had the mind of a man and enjoyed men's company. I did not join in, being content now in my own mind; to my great joy, I had heard from my son Anthony. He had been wounded, but the wound he said was healed. *God be thanked it was not in my hands, but to my thigh in the end; I will be a little lame.* He added that he had been nursed by one of the former Carthusian brothers, now an old man, who had fled with those surviving to Flanders by the end of Henry's reign. They had founded a house there, and would not return to England. All of that seemed far away; and my son wrote little likewise of the horrors of the war. King Philip still desired to assert his rule over the Dutch, but their resistance was stubborn enough to break the greatest king in the world; one could not help but marvel at them and at their leader William of Orange who, like myself, kept silent.

We heard of the loss of Calais to the French. 'That will kill the Queen more swiftly than her abandonment by her husband hath done,' said Kate, smiling and inserting her needle in its velvet. I almost hated her for such heartless sayings. I stood up and went down to the chapel to pray for Mary Tudor and her much-tried heart. When I returned Kate was still at the embroidery, and I said to her, 'Why do you sew and sew at that? You used not to be as apt with the needle.' I sounded as sharp as she did, but I was still sad for the last Catholic Queen of England; her life had held little except disaster. 'Perhaps it is a present for the King in Cracow,' I added more lightly.

The grave eyes raised themselves. 'No,' Kate said, 'it is a present for Queen Elizabeth of England, when the news shall come. Then, we can return.'

So she had made ready. When news of the late Queen's calm death came, Kate sent, by swift messenger, a Yule-gift to Anne Boleyn's daughter; the completed cushion with its pearls, and a copy of the Book of Ecclesiasticus, bound in purple velvet and clasped with silver and gilt.

With it all went a long fulsome letter to the new Queen. If the fires of Smithfield had ever in fact endangered Catharine Willoughby, they would do so no longer. Peregrine would have his English inheritance in due time.

The Cecils were in power, having again turned their coats. *Christ's plain coat without seam is fairer than all the jaggs of Germany,* wrote Kate triumphantly to her friend. There was another saying I had learned long ago from Madame in Flanders; that the greatest wisdom is to be not too wise. We heard various things, firstly that her new Majesty had not waited to hear the Gospel read in church, and that she had put good Bishop White under house arrest for his funeral eulogy which said that the late Queen had been an honest woman. It would have been hard to foresee at that time what was to happen to religion in England; Elizabeth Tudor blew hot and cold then, and there was even talk that she would marry Philip herself, but did not, and he took the King of France's daughter instead, at the peace.

There would be no more open burnings, but many secret tortures and fearful questionings in the Tower; tales of the Marian martyrs have been trumpeted in England, but less is heard of those who suffered later, under Good Queen Bess. For all these reasons, we did not leave Samogitia till 1559, when Her Grace had been a year on the English throne and seemed firmly seated thereon. There were many farewells to be made, for we all knew we would never again see Poland, which had used us kindly.

Then we rode north, towards the sea once more. My son Anthony rode to meet us at Eindhoven in Brabant. His appearance shocked me; he had the face of an older man by far than his years, lined with pain and endurance in the late war. His wound had been more serious than he had ever let me know, for a sword-thrust had pierced his intestines and although by God's mercy the wound had healed, it left him bent and limping, able only with difficulty to mount a horse. However, he was cheerful, with a kind of inner radiance I had not earlier perceived in him. He reminded me of the wounded Basque mercenary Ignatius who, lamed likewise, had withdrawn to a cave for contemplation and had emerged a soldier for God, thereafter teaching himself Latin and attracting followers to form a band of priests unlike any other. It was these Anthony now proposed to join 'if they will have me. They will not take everyone.'

We were in one of the smaller rooms of a

house the Duchess had hired to shelter her family and some of the servants, including both Georges who had come with us; the rest were disposed at inns. I remember going to my son and taking his face between my hands; it so greatly resembled Tom's that tears came into my eyes.

'I am proud of you,' I said. 'It is perhaps the will of God that, after your father failed in the priesthood, you should succeed in his place.' I was certain of Anthony's success in the end; it is a long and arduous training for the Society of Jesus, but he might be otherwise ordained.

He told me that King Philip meant to found a college for priests at Valladolid, his birthplace. 'Come with me to Spain, mother,' he said. 'If you enter England you may not be able to leave again freely; passes now are difficult to obtain. I would have you near me for as long as may be.' He told me that he himself greatly hoped to be sent on the English mission later, and I knew this meant danger; under Cecil, many things had changed, and the country was no longer friendly to the old faith except in certain secret places still.

My son stared out now at the placid Flemish street, quiet again after the war. 'What I learned from King Edward's tutors may service me somewhat in King Philip's seminary,' he said, smiling a little. 'I have not had leisure for scholarship since. Despite the Pope's pardon to England by way of Cardinal

Pole, no more priests are being ordained there, nor I think will be. It is also the will of God that the Cardinal died within two days of Queen Mary; their times had outrun them both. It will be a slower matter to convert England under Cecil and the Queen.' He put Cecil first.

'The Duchess no longer hath need of me,' I said, 'and I am glad to have some measure of your company; we have seen too little of one another over the years.' I thought that perhaps I might help my son with money, a little; I had recovered some in Poland.

'The King will be pleased if you come,' he said. 'He is not the monster the Dutch call him, though the war itself was cruel. His new French bride is young, and he himself hath lost his father. He knows that you were with Madame the Regent at her Court, long ago, and knew Lady Salisbury, of whom he hath heard much. He likes to talk of homely things when he may.' I was to find out later that this was true; King Philip and I talked readily later on to one another about small matters, leaving aside his English marriage; mostly we talked about painting, for he had a particular fancy for a curious artist named Bosch whose pictures he collected, full of strange creatures and odd happenings and colours; perhaps he felt at home with me because I have one blue eye and one brown.

So I went to Spain, with my son; Kate made

no demur, being satisfied with her own homecoming and her welcome by Queen Elizabeth, and the returning of her estates. I did not longer endeavour to fulfil my promise to my father, my duty being now to my son. At first I stayed in a convent in the heart of the Guadarramas, brown as they are in summer and white in winter with the snow. Then the King found me a place about his sister, Princess Juana, most beautiful, so pious that the world had scarcely heard of her, and there with her I could be quiet and remember much. At times a letter would come from Kate in England, not often, but enough to let me know how she fared and who was in her different houses. The Queen, she said, was disgusted with Frances Suffolk's marriage to a groom, as Her Grace called Adrian Stokes, but let the pair live on together at Sheen. Frances's remaining daughters were however less lucky even than poor Jane Grey, who had at least died quickly. The second little girl, Catharine, who had once been proposed for a match with Spain because she was in line to the throne, chose secretly to marry young Hertford without telling the Queen. The bridegroom's sister, Kate related with spice, had to stand guard ouside the door while the marriage of the two young people was hastily consummated in a hired room with a bed. Soon the bride was with child, and on discovery whisked by Elizabeth in anger to the

Tower. Her husband must have contrived to visit her there, as there were three more children born; after that the Queen, hearing of it, parted them completely and for ever. Poor Lady Catharine, having consoled herself with dogs and monkeys for company, died early, and till now, at least, Hertford is still a widower, loving his wife's memory. Mary Grey, the youngest sister, fared even worse; she was a dwarf, and married, again in secret, the largest man at Court, a serjeant-porter well beneath her station. The Queen clapped him in prison, where he was harshly treated; and poor Mary Keynes—she latterly had the courage to sign her name so—was visited on Kate, as little Mary Seymour had long ago been; and, as then, Kate complained bitterly about the expense of keeping her. 'She is greatly ashamed of her fault,' she wrote to me, adding that Lady Mary had only brought two pillows with her, one longer than the other, and not much else. 'What fault is that?' I wrote back boldly, ignoring the matter of pillows. 'She married where she loved. Others have done the same.'

This was a barb, for Kate's marriage to Bertie had given offence to the high nobility, and the Queen refused him the title of Lord Willoughby because of his low birth, despite King Ethelred. Kate had tried hard to obtain the title for him, but it will no doubt go to Peregrine. He, I believe, is handsome; so much so that Bess of Hardwick's daughter, among others, fell in love with him, but Peregrine had no fancy for her, and soon she married, again in secret—how hard it is on all these loving young folk!—none other than Madge Lennox's last surviving son, Lord Charles Stuart, as they spell it now. Poor Madge was sent to the Tower for her part in it, where as she wrote she had been three times for love; once for Tom Howard long ago, a second time for the marriage of her son Darnley to the Queen of Scots, ending in his murder; and now thirdly on account of Elizabeth Cavendish and young Charles, both of whom soon died leaving a daughter, Lady Arbell. Madge's husband Lennox, whom she had loved well, was murdered also, in Scotland; their grandson now is King. He may well inherit the double throne, though they say his tongue is too big for his mouth; the Queen of England will neither make heirs nor name them. She hath imprisoned his mother long ago. Tudor jealousy is as much alive as it was in the days of the de la Poles and poor Warwick; that I should have lived to remember it all! Kate and Bertie, however, continue happy together.

* * *

Ay, I am old. Nevertheless, I am glad that my Anthony may be ordered to the English mission, albeit more dangerous than ever now the Pope has excommunicated the Queen. That I think was a mistake; priests accordingly in England are used even more hardly than before, arrested and done to death like so many long ago in the Pilgrimage of Grace, the Carthusians, the rest. That my son should be a martyr I dare not pray; but I pray nevertheless daily for his welfare, staring at my fair-haired Princess before me quietly kneeling at her prie-dieu, most of the day. Pain refines men, and women also. I have known much pain, some love, many places and people. Soon now I shall meet with God, when all things will be known.

We hope you have enjoyed this Large Print book. Other Chivers Press or Thorndike Press Large Print books are available at your library or directly from the publishers.

For more information about current and forthcoming titles, please call or write, without obligation, to:

Chivers Large Print
published by BBC Audiobooks Ltd
St James House, The Square
Lower Bristol Road
Bath BA2 3BH
UK
email: bbcaudiobooks@bbc.co.uk
www.bbcaudiobooks.co.uk

OR

Thorndike Press
295 Kennedy Memorial Drive
Waterville
Maine 04901
USA
www.gale.com/thorndike
www.gale.com/wheeler

All our Large Print titles are designed for easy reading, and all our books are made to last.